YOUNG REBELS, your emotions are like a fire. When controlled, they are useful; when uncontrolled, they are damaging. **HEREIN** you will learn the secret to controlling your emotions. **YOUR REBELLIOUS HEART** can be *renewed* if **YOUR MIND** is *receptive* to the help.

IS THERE A REBEL IN THE HOUSE?
Youth Overcoming a Rebellious Heart

Edward D. Andrews

IS THERE A REBEL IN THE HOUSE

Youth Overcoming a Rebellious Heart

Edward D. Andrews

Christian Publishing House
Cambridge, Ohio

Copyright © 2017 Edward D. Andrews

All rights reserved. Except for brief quotations in articles, other publications, book reviews, and blogs, no part of this book may be reproduced in any manner without prior written permission from the publishers. For information, write, support@christianpublishers.org

Unless otherwise stated, Scripture quotations are from Updated American Standard Version (UASV) Copyright © 2022 by Christian Publishing House

IS THERE A REBEL IN THE HOUSE: Youth Overcoming a Rebellious Heart by Edward D. Andrews

ISBN-10: 1945757396

ISBN-13: 978-1945757396

Table of Contents

Book Description 6

Preface 8

Introduction 10

CHAPTER 1 Learning from Jesus' Illustration 12

CHAPTER 2 What Is a Rebel? 16

CHAPTER 3 Causes of Rebellion 20

CHAPTER 4 Permissive Parenting and Overly Restrictive Parenting 26

CHAPTER 5 Providing Your Child with the Basic Needs Can Prevent Rebellion 33

CHAPTER 6 When Children Get Into Difficulty 41

CHAPTER 7 Handling a Determined Rebel 51

CHAPTER 8 Bible Principles that Can Help Parents Prevent Serious Rebellion 58

CHAPTER 9 Help Your Teenager to Thrive 64

CHAPTER 10 Honest and Open Communication 69

CHAPTER 11 What You Should Communicate 78

CHAPTER 12 Discipline and Respect 90

CHAPTER 13 Work and Recreation for Teenagers 97

CHAPTER 14 From Teenager to Adult 103

Edward D. Andrews

Book Description

In a world where the sanctity of the home is continually under attack, and rebellion among youth is not only commonplace but often even celebrated, "IS THERE A REBEL IN THE HOUSE?: Youth Overcoming a Rebellious Heart" serves as a timely guide for parents seeking Biblical wisdom on raising children with godly character. Drawing from a wealth of Scriptural principles, this book offers comprehensive insights into the dynamics that contribute to rebellion, while providing actionable solutions for both prevention and intervention.

Starting with the foundational teachings of Jesus, this book delves into the anatomy of rebellion—exploring its causes, identifying its symptoms, and demystifying the factors that often contribute to a rebellious heart. It discusses the consequences of varying parenting styles, from the perils of permissiveness to the pitfalls of overly restrictive parenting, and sheds light on how meeting a child's basic needs can serve as a safeguard against rebellion.

Navigating the treacherous waters of adolescence, the book goes on to explore effective ways of handling children who have already taken a rebellious path. With its strong emphasis on the role of Scriptural principles, it equips parents with the tools they need to correct misbehavior without exacerbating the problem.

"IS THERE A REBEL IN THE HOUSE?" isn't just about crisis management; it's about raising resilient, responsible, and God-fearing individuals. With chapters dedicated to helping your teenager thrive and facilitating honest and open communication, it addresses the essential elements that contribute to a healthy parent-child relationship. The book also dives deep into topics such as discipline, respect, work ethics, and the crucial transition from teenager to adult.

Whether you're struggling with a rebellious child or simply wish to instill strong Christian values in your family, this book offers a roadmap to guide you through the challenges and joys of Christian parenting. Secure your family's spiritual legacy by harnessing the power of Scriptural wisdom to overcome rebellion and raise God-honoring adults.

Edward D. Andrews

Preface

Dear Reader,

As you find yourself holding this book, it's likely that you're either facing the challenge of dealing with a rebellious young heart in your home, or you're taking proactive steps to prevent rebellion from sprouting in the first place. Either way, I commend you for seeking guidance grounded in the Scriptures.

Our society often glamorizes rebellion as a rite of passage or an expression of individuality, yet the Bible paints a different picture altogether. The young prodigal son's story in the Scriptures serves as a poignant example of how rebellion can lead to devastating consequences. As such, it's crucial that we view the problem through a Biblical lens, for therein lies the path to true solutions.

This book is not a theoretical exploration but an actionable guide designed to bring Scriptural wisdom into the everyday challenges of parenting. While it provides an in-depth understanding of what rebellion is and its various causes, the book goes beyond mere diagnosis. It offers both preventive and corrective measures based on Biblical principles that have stood the test of time.

I must emphasize that this book does not promise a quick fix. Parenting, as you may already know, is a journey filled with twists and turns. The key to effective parenting, however, is consistent application of Scriptural principles in nurturing, disciplining, and guiding your child's character.

You will find that the chapters are organized in a way that starts with understanding the root of rebellion, followed by strategies for prevention, and then intervention methods for more severe cases. This flow aims to offer a comprehensive view of the issue, along with a systematic approach to tackle it.

It is my fervent prayer that this book serves as a valuable resource, fortifying your family's spiritual well-being and offering you the tools to raise children who are not only obedient to you but also to God. As you read through these pages, may you be encouraged, inspired, and above all, equipped to guide your child's heart toward the eternal wisdom that is found only in God's Word.

In His Service,

Edward D. Andrews

Author of 220+ books and Chief Translator of the Updated American Standard Version

Edward D. Andrews

Introduction

Welcome to a transformative journey aimed at not only understanding but also effectively dealing with one of the most challenging aspects of parenting: a rebellious heart in our youth. While the Preface offered you an overview of the overarching vision of this book, this Introduction serves to set the stage for what lies ahead in the ensuing chapters. The aim is to equip you with the foundational perspective that is necessary to engage with the content in a meaningful and actionable way.

Why This Book Is Important

Rebellion isn't just an annoying habit or a phase that children "grow out of"; it is a serious concern that can have long-lasting consequences, both spiritually and relationally. The Bible is clear on the importance of obedience to authority and how rebellion is tantamount to the "sin of divination" (1 Samuel 15:23). When left unaddressed, a rebellious heart can set a child on a dangerous path, far from the guidance of God and the loving influence of family.

Bridging the Gap: Faith and Parenting

Many books on parenting offer practical tips and psychological insights, but few align these insights with the eternal wisdom of the Scriptures. This book aims to fill that gap by fusing Biblical principles with real-world parenting strategies. Here, the wisdom of the Bible isn't an add-on; it is the core foundation on which every piece of advice and every strategy is built.

A Multi-Faceted Approach

We begin with defining rebellion from a Biblical standpoint in **Chapter 2**, "What Is a Rebel?". This helps lay the groundwork for understanding the issue at its root. Then, we delve into its various causes in **Chapter 3**, "Causes of Rebellion", before discussing the pitfalls of permissive and overly restrictive parenting in **Chapter 4**.

As we move forward, the book shifts from understanding rebellion to preventing and dealing with it. While **Chapter 5** provides strategies for meeting basic child needs to ward off rebellion, **Chapter 6** and **Chapter 7** offer targeted advice for those challenging times when children do get into difficulty or show persistent signs of a rebellious heart.

Finally, we explore how to fortify your home against serious rebellion through Bible principles and how to help your teenager thrive in a God-honoring way, in **Chapters 8 and 9**. The last section of the book provides hands-on advice about communication, discipline, work, recreation, and transition from adolescence to adulthood.

Not a Monologue, but a Dialogue

This book is not just a set of commandments etched in stone; consider it more as a guide for an ongoing dialogue between you, your child, and most importantly, Jehovah. As you read, pause to reflect on how the Biblical principles relate to your specific circumstances, perhaps even jot down notes or questions for further study and discussion within your family.

With that said, let's embark on this transformative journey together. As you turn the page to the first chapter, may you open not just a book, but a new chapter in your family's spiritual life.

Edward D. Andrews

CHAPTER 1 Learning from Jesus' Illustration

The Parable of the Wicked Tenants: An Illustration of Jewish Leaders' Unfaithfulness

Jesus often used parables as a teaching tool to highlight spiritual truths. One such parable that specifically addresses the unfaithfulness of the Jewish religious leaders of His day is the Parable of the Wicked Tenants, recorded in the Gospels of Matthew, Mark, and Luke. In Matthew 21:33-46, we read this parable, where a landowner plants a vineyard, puts a wall around it, digs a winepress, and builds a tower. He then rents the vineyard to some farmers and goes away on a journey.

The Rejection of the Landowner's Messengers

In this parable, the landowner sends servants to collect the fruit that was rightfully his. However, the tenants mistreat the servants; some are beaten, some killed. The landowner then decides to send his son, thinking the tenants would respect him. *This action of sending the son symbolizes God sending Jesus Christ, His beloved Son*, to the Jewish people.

The Unfaithfulness Exemplified

Shockingly, the tenants plot to kill the son, assuming that they would inherit the vineyard if he is out of the picture. They seize him, throw him out of the vineyard, and kill him. Here, the unfaithfulness of the Jewish religious leaders is laid bare. They were entrusted with the spiritual well-being of God's chosen people but proved to be self-serving and faithless. Jesus ends the parable by asking, "Therefore, when the owner of the vineyard comes, what will he do to those tenants?" The Pharisees themselves pronounce the judgment, stating that the wicked tenants should be destroyed, and the vineyard given to others who would produce its fruits (Matthew 21:40-41).

The Cornerstone and The Judgment

Jesus then quotes Psalm 118:22-23 about the stone the builders rejected becoming the cornerstone. He makes it clear that the kingdom of God will be taken from them and given to a people producing its fruits (Matthew 21:43). *The Pharisees and the chief priests realized Jesus was talking about them* (Matthew 21:45). Here, Jesus prophetically foretells the destruction of the temple and the dispersion of the Jewish people, further solidifying that the custodianship of God's revelation would be transferred to another group—those who would accept Jesus as the Messiah and Savior.

Implications for Us Today

While this parable is historically focused on the unfaithfulness of the Jewish religious leaders of Jesus' day, it also serves as a cautionary tale for all religious leaders in every era. Leaders are entrusted with the spiritual well-being of their flock, and God will hold them accountable for how they handle this sacred responsibility. Hebrews 13:17 reminds us, "Obey your leaders and submit to them, for they are keeping watch over your souls, as those who will have to give an account."

The Parable of the Wicked Tenants serves as a profound illustration of the failure of the Jewish religious leaders to fulfill their God-given role. Their unfaithfulness was not only a betrayal of their immediate responsibilities but also had eternal implications, as it led to the rejection of Jesus, the Messiah they had been awaiting.

The Parable of the Wicked Tenants: Understanding Adolescents in the Context of Unfaithfulness

The Parable of the Wicked Tenants (Matthew 21:33-46; Mark 12:1-12; Luke 20:9-19) is primarily an indictment of the Jewish religious leaders of Jesus' time. In this parable, tenants are entrusted with a vineyard but refuse to give the owner his due. They even go to the extent of killing the son of the owner. Jesus' message was clear: the religious leaders had been entrusted with the spiritual care of Israel, but they had failed in their duties and would face judgment.

The Relevance to Adolescents

While the primary focus is not on adolescence, we can draw out principles that may be applicable. Here's how:

1. **Respect for Authority**: The tenants demonstrate a glaring lack of respect for the authority over them, a trait often exhibited by rebellious adolescents. They reject the vineyard owner's messengers and even his son, similar to how some adolescents may reject the teachings and guidance of their parents or other figures of authority.

2. **Consequences for Actions**: The parable ends with severe consequences for the wicked tenants. This underscores the Biblical principle that actions have consequences, a critical lesson for adolescents to grasp.

3. **The Importance of Right Choices**: The tenants made a series of wrong choices that led them down the path of destruction. Adolescence is a time of significant decision-making that can set the trajectory for the rest of one's life. Learning to make wise, Biblically-informed decisions is crucial.

4. **Role of Guiding Figures**: The tenants disregarded the vineyard owner, who rightfully expected fruit from his vineyard. Likewise, parents and spiritual leaders are like the vineyard owners expecting "spiritual fruits" from their children. It shows that guidance and wisdom from trusted elders should not be disregarded.

5. **Entitlement Versus Responsibility**: The tenants felt entitled to take over the vineyard, ignoring their responsibility to the owner. Adolescents may also struggle with feelings of entitlement, which can be tempered by teachings on responsibility and accountability.

Countering the Rebel Heart with Scripture

A teenager equipped with the wisdom of Scripture, understanding the importance of authority, responsibility, and the consequences of choices, is better prepared to face the challenges of adolescence. Such a teen is less likely to harbor a "rebellious heart" as mentioned in our book "IS THERE A REBEL IN THE HOUSE?: Youth Overcoming a Rebellious Heart."

To that end, parents should employ passages such as Ephesians 6:1-3 ("Children, obey your parents in the Lord, for this is right") and Proverbs 1:8-9 ("Listen, my son, to your father's instruction and do not forsake your mother's teaching") to educate their adolescents about the importance of respecting authority and making wise decisions.

While the Parable of the Wicked Tenants is not directly about adolescents, the principles derived from it serve as powerful lessons for young people. Adolescence, a formative period, can be better navigated when guided by the immutable truths of Scripture. It's crucial for parents and spiritual mentors to employ Biblical truths when steering young souls through this tumultuous phase.

CHAPTER 2 What Is a Rebel?

Understanding the Term "Rebel"

The term "rebel" originates from the Latin word "rebellis," which means "waging war again; insurgent." In a Scriptural context, rebellion is essentially a deliberate and intentional act of defiance against established authority. In 1 Samuel 15:23, the prophet Samuel told King Saul, "For rebellion is as the sin of divination, and presumption is as iniquity and idolatry." This emphasizes that rebellion in the eyes of God is as serious as idolatry and divination. The prophet Isaiah also speaks of the rebellious nature of Israel: "Ah, sinful nation, a people laden with iniquity, offspring of evildoers, children who deal corruptly! They have forsaken Jehovah, they have despised the Holy One of Israel, they are utterly estranged" (Isaiah 1:4).

The Danger of Hasty Labeling

While understanding the seriousness of rebellion from a Scriptural standpoint is vital, parents should exercise extreme caution before labeling their child as a rebel. Here are several reasons why:

Misinterpretation of Developmental Behavior

Children go through various developmental stages where they test boundaries as a natural part of growing up. Labeling this curiosity or boundary-testing as "rebellion" could mischaracterize a child's behavior. Parents should discern whether the actions are age-appropriate explorations or intentional acts of defiance.

Emotional and Psychological Impact

Once a child is labeled a rebel, this title can become a self-fulfilling prophecy. A child might start to act according to the negative label they have been assigned, which can be emotionally and psychologically damaging in the long run.

Impedes Constructive Dialogue

If parents hastily label their child a rebel, this can shut down any open lines of communication. The child may feel misunderstood and cornered, making them less likely to engage in constructive dialogue about what they're experiencing or why they acted a certain way.

Potential for Grace and Transformation

Scripture is replete with examples of individuals who might have been considered "rebels" but later turned their hearts toward God. The Apostle Paul is a prime example; he persecuted Christians before his encounter with Christ (Acts 9:1-19). Therefore, there is always room for grace, transformation, and redemption.

While rebellion is a grave matter that shouldn't be taken lightly, labeling a child a rebel is a significant step that should be taken with caution and discernment. Parents should carefully evaluate the nature of the behavior, consult Scripture, and seek wisdom in prayer before making such a weighty judgment.

The Occasional Disobedience: An Overview

When parents find themselves in a situation where their teenager is occasionally disobedient, it can be a challenging period that tests their patience and understanding. However, it is important for parents to bear several key principles in mind during such times.

Contextualize the Disobedience

Firstly, it is crucial to understand that occasional disobedience does not necessarily constitute rebellion. The Apostle Paul highlights that "all have sinned and fall short of the glory of God" (Romans 3:23). Therefore, occasional disobedience may just be a manifestation of the sinful nature that every human possesses, and not a rebellious heart.

Emotional and Psychological Changes

Teenagers are at a stage of life where they are undergoing rapid emotional and psychological changes. The Bible acknowledges the different stages of human development; even Jesus Christ "increased in wisdom and in stature and in favor with God and man" (Luke 2:52). With hormones raging and their search for an identity in full swing, occasional disobedience might be a byproduct of their developmental stage.

Practical Considerations for Parents

Exercise Patience and Compassion

Remember the Scriptural injunction, "Fathers, do not provoke your children to anger, but bring them up in the discipline and instruction of the Lord" (Ephesians 6:4). Parents should not let occasional disobedience lead to an environment of hostility and perpetual discipline, but exercise patience and compassion.

Maintain Open Communication

Having open lines of communication can alleviate misunderstandings and provide insights into the reason behind the disobedience. Solomon advises, "The purpose in a man's heart is like deep water, but a man of understanding will draw it out" (Proverbs 20:5).

Encourage Godly Wisdom

While teenagers may act out from time to time, this is an opportunity to instill godly wisdom in their hearts. Proverbs 22:6 instructs, "Train up a child in the way he should go; even when he is old he will not depart from it."

Occasional disobedience from a teenager should not be hastily equated with a rebellious heart. Parents need to view such instances in the light of Scriptural wisdom, the developmental stage of adolescence, and the emotional complexities that come with it. By maintaining open communication and utilizing these occasions as teaching moments, parents can guide their teenagers toward godly wisdom and maturity.

CHAPTER 3 Causes of Rebellion

The Satanic Environment: A Catalyst for Rebellion

We must acknowledge that we live in a world where Satan, described as the "god of this world," has blinded the minds of unbelievers (2 Corinthians 4:4). It is not merely a metaphorical description but a warning about the tangible impact Satan and his system can have on our lives, including the lives of our children.

The Lure of Worldly Ideologies

In an environment saturated with secularism, hedonism, and materialism, children are constantly bombarded with messages that are antithetical to Christian teachings. The Apostle John cautions us: "Do not love the world or the things in the world. If anyone loves the world, the love of the Father is not in him" (1 John 2:15). These worldly ideologies can foster rebellion as they undermine godly principles.

The Role of Peer Pressure

Peer pressure can serve as a conduit for satanic influence. In Proverbs, we find a warning against succumbing to peer pressure: "My son, if sinners entice you, do not consent" (Proverbs 1:10). A child spending time with a circle that promotes disobedience, disrespect, or other sinful behaviors may find himself lured into rebelling against godly authority.

Media and Entertainment

Satan also utilizes the media and entertainment industry to infiltrate young minds. Paul warns, "Whatever is true, whatever is honorable, whatever is just, whatever is pure, whatever is lovely, whatever is commendable, if there is any excellence, if there is anything worthy of praise, think about these things" (Philippians 4:8). The types of music, movies, and games a child interacts with can either build them up in righteousness or lead them down the path of rebellion.

Counteracting the Satanic Environment

Daily Spiritual Nourishment

Providing daily spiritual nourishment through family worship, Bible reading, and prayer can serve as a shield. Jesus himself said, "Man shall not live by bread alone, but by every word that comes from the mouth of God" (Matthew 4:4).

Be the Godly Example

Children are more likely to follow what they see rather than just what they hear. A parent should strive to be the embodiment of godly living. Paul exhorts, "Be imitators of me, as I am of Christ" (1 Corinthians 11:1).

Community Support

It is often said, "It takes a village to raise a child," and this couldn't be truer in a spiritual sense. A supportive church community can be invaluable. The Bible speaks of mutual edification (1 Thessalonians 5:11) and the importance of corporate worship (Hebrews 10:25), which can serve as a bulwark against satanic influence.

The satanic environment we live in can significantly influence a child towards rebellion, acting against their parents and ultimately against God. However, the influences of worldly ideologies, peer pressure, and media can be counteracted through daily spiritual nourishment, a godly example set by parents, and a strong community of believers. These preventative measures not only offer protection but also equip the child with the spiritual armor needed to face the battles ahead.

The Inclination Toward Rebellion: A Multifaceted Issue

Understanding the factors that might lead to rebellion in a child is complex and requires a nuanced approach rooted in Scriptural insight.

Innate Sinful Nature

Genesis 6:5 reveals that "the wickedness of man was great in the earth, and that every intention of the thoughts of his heart was only evil continually." Again, after the flood, God acknowledges in Genesis 8:21 that "the intention of man's heart is evil from his youth." These Scriptures indicate that humans are born with an innate sinful nature, mentally bent toward evil.

Similarly, Jeremiah 17:9 states, "The heart [inner person] is deceitful above all things, and desperately sick; who can understand it?" This Scriptural diagnosis of the human heart is a stern reminder that children, too, carry this inner deceit and sickness.

Paul also lends his voice to this discussion in Romans 7:18-19, "For I know that nothing good dwells in me, that is, in my flesh. For I have the desire to do what is right, but not the ability to carry it out. For I do not do the good I want, but the evil I do not want is what I keep on doing."

Developmental Considerations

Scientific research shows that the human brain is not fully developed until around 25 years of age. This means that the young, impressionable minds are extremely susceptible to influences—both good and bad. In a world where they are bombarded by all sorts of messages, this developmental stage makes them particularly vulnerable.

Factors Leading to Rebellion

Lack of Proper Guidance

In a world filled with so much confusion and moral relativism, the absence of clear, godly guidance can make a child more susceptible to rebellion. "Train up a child in the way he should go; even when he is old he will not depart from it" (Proverbs 22:6).

Peer Influence

As mentioned, children and adolescents are highly susceptible to peer influence. The yearning for acceptance and belonging can sometimes make them choose the path of least resistance, which often is the path leading away from God (Proverbs 1:10-15).

Emotional and Psychological Struggles

At times, emotional pain, unaddressed psychological issues, or a lack of self-worth can manifest as rebellion.

Lack of Discipline

Hebrews 12:11 reminds us that "For the moment all discipline seems painful rather than pleasant, but later it yields the peaceful fruit of righteousness to those who have been trained by it." A lack of discipline can serve as a fertile ground for nurturing a rebellious spirit.

Exposure to Unhealthy Media and Culture

Unfiltered access to media and pop culture that promote values contrary to Christian living can lead to rebellion (Philippians 4:8).

The factors that can lead to rebellion in a child are numerous and interconnected. The child's innate sinful nature, coupled with the vulnerabilities that come with undeveloped cognitive faculties, sets the stage. Additional factors such as peer pressure, emotional struggles, lack of discipline, and exposure to ungodly influences can then push the child further down the path of rebellion. Parents and guardians, therefore, have the significant responsibility to counter these factors with Scriptural teachings, godly discipline, and loving guidance.

The Complexity of Child Rebellion: Beyond Immediate Triggers

While we have previously discussed some common factors contributing to child rebellion, it is essential to recognize that the causes can be both varied and deeply rooted. There are other less-evident, but significant factors that could potentially drive a child toward rebellious behavior.

A Toxic Home Environment

An unstable home environment can have a detrimental impact on a child's emotional and spiritual health. If a parent engages in substance abuse, be it alcohol or drugs, or displays violent tendencies toward the other parent, the emotional toll on a child can be enormous. Such environments warp the child's view of life and of what is normal, and this can result in a form of rebellion that is actually a cry for help or stability.

Parental Neglect

Even in homes that appear stable, a child may rebel because he or she feels neglected or unimportant to the parents. This absence of emotional connection can be a potent catalyst for rebellion. "Fathers, do not provoke your children to anger, but bring them up in the discipline and instruction of the Lord" (Ephesians 6:4).

The Impact of Human Imperfection

Romans 5:12 states, "Therefore, just as through one man [Adam] sin entered into the world, and death through sin, and so death spread to all men, because all sinned." The rebelliousness that we observe in youths might not always be triggered by external influences or bad parenting. It could very well be an internal struggle stemming from the inherent sinful nature passed down through Adam. The Apostle Paul reminds us of this dark heritage, which implies that some youths may choose rebellion simply because human imperfection is deeply ingrained within them. Adam was, in essence, the first rebel, and we have all inherited his legacy of rebellion to some extent.

A Conscious Choice to Rebel

In some instances, rebellion is an active, willful decision. Even children who have been raised in godly homes, well-sheltered from the harmful influences of the world, may choose to rebel. This is perhaps the most painful situation for parents who have done their best to "train up a child in the way he should go" (Proverbs 22:6), only to see him choose a different path. This mirrors the rebellion of Adam, who was placed in a perfect environment yet still chose to rebel against God.

Rebellion in children and youths can arise from various factors, ranging from a toxic home environment and parental neglect to deeply-rooted human imperfection. Sometimes, despite a family's best efforts to instill godly values, a child may make a deliberate choice to rebel. Recognizing these complexities can help parents and spiritual leaders to deal more effectively with rebellion when it occurs, relying always on the wisdom and guidance of Scripture to navigate these challenging circumstances.

Edward D. Andrews

CHAPTER 4 Permissive Parenting and Overly Restrictive Parenting

The Perils of Extremes in Child Rearing: Striking the Biblical Balance

Child-rearing is one of the most challenging responsibilities that parents undertake, and it's fraught with opportunities for imbalance. Scripture advises against provoking our children, as this can lead them to discouragement or rebellion (Colossians 3:21). The pitfalls often lie at the extremes—either being too restrictive or too permissive. Let's delve into these dangerous inclinations, drawing insights from Biblical examples.

Overly Restrictive Parenting: The Dangers of Excessive Control

Some parents, with the best of intentions, impose excessive rules, limitations, and disciplines on their children. While discipline is a Biblical principle ("Whoever spares the rod hates his son, but he who loves him is diligent to discipline him," Proverbs 13:24), excessive control can stifle a child's growth and sense of agency. This can lead to resentment and rebellion as the child seeks freedom and autonomy.

Biblical Example: The Pharisees

Though not a direct parallel, the example of the Pharisees can serve as a warning against overly restrictive religious environments. The Pharisees were known for their excessive legalism, adding human rules to the Mosaic Law, which resulted in a burdensome yoke on the people (Matthew 23:4). The rigidity of their system led not to greater righteousness but to hypocrisy and spiritual blindness.

Overly Permissive Parenting: The Dangers of Laxity

At the other end of the spectrum are parents who provide little to no boundaries for their children. This form of parenting fails to provide the guidance and structure that children need to develop moral and ethical principles. Without discipline and correction, a child lacks the necessary framework for responsible behavior, leading to poor choices and, often, rebellion.

Biblical Example: Eli and His Sons

Eli, the high priest, serves as a warning against permissive parenting. His sons, Hophni and Phinehas, were wicked men who did not know God, stealing from the sacrifices and committing immoral acts (1 Samuel 2:12-17). Despite their flagrant disobedience, Eli failed to restrain or correct them adequately, leading to disastrous consequences for the family and the nation (1 Samuel 3:11-14).

Striving for Balance: Recognizing Individual Needs

Different children have different temperaments and needs. What works for one child may not work for another, requiring a discerning approach that balances discipline with grace. The Apostle Paul's counsel to fathers to avoid exasperating their children but to bring them up in the "discipline and instruction of the Lord" (Ephesians 6:4) captures the essence of balanced parenting. This involves not just rules but also love, instruction, and the cultivation of a relationship that mirrors the love of our heavenly Father.

Extreme approaches in child-rearing—whether overly restrictive or overly permissive—can provoke a child to rebellion. Striking a balance is critical but challenging, as each child is unique. The Biblical examples caution us against these extremes and encourage us to employ a balanced approach rooted in Biblical wisdom and discernment.

Eli the High Priest: A Cautionary Tale for Christian Parents

While Eli was a longstanding and likely faithful high priest of Israel, his record as a parent leaves much to be desired. There are crucial lessons that modern-day parents can learn from Eli's failures in child-rearing, particularly regarding the discipline and spiritual instruction of children.

Eli's Misguided Permissiveness: Honoring Children Over God

Eli's sons, Hophni and Phinehas, were "good-for-nothing men," who disregarded the sacredness of their duties and indulged in immoral and sacrilegious behavior (1 Samuel 2:12-17). Although Eli was no doubt aware of the Law of God and probably even instructed his sons in it, he failed in one critical aspect of parenting: discipline.

Instead of taking decisive action against his sons' vile conduct, Eli offered only a feeble rebuke. He did not remove them from their roles as officiating priests, which would have been a just consequence for their egregious sins. By failing to enact significant disciplinary action, Eli honored his sons more than he honored God. This grave mistake led not only to the rebellion of his sons but also to calamity upon his entire house (1 Samuel 3:13-14; 4:11-22).

Spiritual Indulgence as a Form of Disobedience

It's vital to note that by not disciplining his sons, Eli was, in essence, rebelling against God's standards. His permissiveness was not merely a lack of discipline but a failure to uphold the holiness and righteousness of God, a requirement of his high position.

Consequently, his entire household suffered the direct consequences of that disobedience.

The Dangers of Withholding Discipline

Eli's permissive parenting underscores the inherent dangers of withholding discipline, as pointed out by Proverbs 29:21, "A servant pampered from youth will bring grief in the end." In Eli's case, his adult sons became corrupt precisely because discipline was lacking in their upbringing.

Confusing Love with Permissiveness

One of the most damaging misconceptions that can befall a parent is the confusion of love with permissiveness. Some parents might think that setting and enforcing rules is unloving, but Scripture teaches otherwise. Eli's feeble attempts at rebuke did nothing to change his sons' behavior, highlighting the danger of failing to enforce godly principles through meaningful discipline.

When discipline is consistently withheld, the consequence can be dire: "Because the sentence against an evil deed is not executed speedily, the heart of the children of man is fully set to do evil" (Ecclesiastes 8:11). A lack of timely and appropriate discipline can embolden a child to further disobedience, as it sends the message that actions don't have consequences.

What Parents Can Learn from Eli

1. **Prioritize God Over Emotional Attachments**: Parents must be willing to discipline their children out of a commitment to uphold godly standards, even when it is emotionally challenging.
2. **Do Not Confuse Love with Permissiveness**: Genuine love disciplines and corrects, guiding children towards righteousness (Hebrews 12:6).

3. **Be Consistent in Discipline**: Sporadic or inconsequential discipline confuses children and fails to instill proper respect for authority.
4. **Uphold God's Standards in the Home**: As spiritual leaders in the home, parents have a responsibility to enact rules and discipline that are aligned with Scripture, modeling these principles through their own behavior.

Eli serves as a cautionary tale, illuminating the serious repercussions of parental permissiveness. Parents must not only teach their children the principles of God's word but must also have the courage to enforce these principles through consistent, loving discipline. Failure to do so can lead to spiritual rebellion and calamity, making this a matter of utmost spiritual urgency.

Rehoboam's Failure in Leadership: Lessons in Parenting from a Divided Kingdom

The story of Rehoboam, the son of Solomon and the last king to rule over a united Israel, serves as a strong example of what not to do in a position of authority, especially for parents striving to raise their children in a godly manner.

Rehoboam's Missteps: Ignoring Wise Counsel and Imposing Heavy Burdens

Rehoboam found himself at the helm of a discontented nation, largely due to the oppressive policies of his father, Solomon. A delegation came to him, asking for a lightening of these burdens. However, rather than heeding the wise counsel of his elder advisors, Rehoboam chose arrogance and pride, imposing even harsher measures on the people. This led to a rebellion, resulting in the division of the kingdom into the northern and southern tribes (1 Kings 12:1-21; 2 Chronicles 10:19).

The Downfall of Ignoring Wise Counsel

One of the most glaring mistakes Rehoboam made was his failure to listen to mature advice. Proverbs 12:15 reminds us, "The way of a fool is right in his own eyes, but a wise man listens to advice." Rehoboam's arrogance clouded his judgment, which was a catastrophic failure in leadership.

The Spiritual Imperative of Seeking God's Guidance

To avoid such pitfalls, parents need to "search for God" in prayer and consistently examine their child-rearing practices in light of Biblical principles (Psalm 105:4). **Prayer and Scripture are not optional supplements; they are essential components of wise parenting.**

The Dangers of Oppressive Parenting

"Mere oppression may make a wise one act crazy," warns Ecclesiastes 7:7. If parents make the atmosphere in the home so rigid that it stifles the child's growth and development, they are laying the groundwork for rebellion. This was the essence of Rehoboam's mistake; he imposed burdens instead of administering fair governance.

The Balance Between Fair Latitude and Firm Boundaries

Children, particularly adolescents, need well-thought-out boundaries that both protect them and allow room for growth. They should not live in an environment so restrictive that it hinders the development of self-reliance and self-confidence. Balanced boundaries create a secure framework within which children can explore, learn, and mature. Most teenagers will feel less inclined to rebel when they experience a balanced mix of freedom and structure.

Lessons Parents Can Learn from Rehoboam

1. **Seek God in Prayer and Scripture**: Always consult God's word and pray for wisdom in your parenting decisions.

2. **Heed Wise Counsel**: Whether from Scripture or mature Christians, wise counsel should not be ignored. The counsel may provide the perspective you lack.

3. **Avoid Oppressive Measures**: Ecclesiastes 7:7 cautions against the damaging effects of oppression, which can provoke even a wise person to act irrationally.

4. **Strive for Balanced Boundaries**: Create an environment that is neither too lax nor too restrictive, allowing your children to develop necessary life skills and spiritual qualities.

In summary, Rehoboam's example stands as a cautionary tale for all those who wield authority, especially parents. It's crucial to avoid the extremes of oppressive rigidity and reckless permissiveness by seeking God's guidance and applying Biblical principles to parenting. This balanced approach will usually result in a less rebellious spirit among teenagers and a more harmonious Christian home.

CHAPTER 5 Providing Your Child with the Basic Needs Can Prevent Rebellion

Viewing Child Development Through a Biblical Lens: Balancing Independence and Stability

The task of parenting is indeed one of the most rewarding yet challenging roles anyone can undertake. As children grow, parents often find themselves in a tricky balance of rejoicing over each milestone while grappling with the uncertainties that each developmental stage presents.

The Natural Transition to Self-Reliance

Christian parents, in particular, may find the adolescent phase somewhat daunting, as children transition from dependence to a form of self-reliance. This can be an emotionally charged period, filled with moments of stubbornness or uncooperativeness. However, it is crucial to remember that the end goal is to raise a mature, stable, and responsible Christian. **The ultimate goal is not just physical growth but spiritual and emotional maturity.** The Scriptures encourage believers to grow in every way, as seen in 1 Corinthians 13:11 and Ephesians 4:13-14, which admonish believers to mature in their understanding and not be "tossed to and fro" by every wind of doctrine.

Understanding Adolescents' Need for Independence

Parents must be cautious not to react negatively every time their adolescent child asks for more independence. As difficult as this may be, especially for those who have protected their child through infancy and childhood, it's essential to recognize that independence is a natural part of human development. **This period of growing independence is not rebellion; rather, it's a necessary phase for developing into a functional adult.**

The Example of Young King Josiah

Consider the example of young King Josiah. At about the age of 15, Josiah began to earnestly seek Jehovah, the God of David, according to 2 Chronicles 34:1-3. This was not a trivial quest but a life-changing, nation-impacting endeavor. Josiah was clearly a responsible young man who was fully capable of making critical life decisions. He exemplifies what can happen when young people are given the room to grow and develop in a balanced manner, both spiritually and personally.

Practical Steps for Parents: Meeting Basic Needs as a Preventive Measure Against Rebellion

1. **Encourage Spiritual Exploration**: Allow your teenager the freedom to explore their faith independently, which can mean personal Bible study or even involvement in Christian activities that they choose themselves.

2. **Provide Emotional Support**: The teenage years are filled with emotional ups and downs. Emotional support, grounded in Christian love, can go a long way in helping them navigate these turbulent years.

3. **Foster Responsible Behavior**: This can be through chores, part-time jobs, or volunteering. Responsibility cultivates maturity.

4. **Set Realistic Boundaries**: While it's crucial to allow your adolescent room to grow, boundaries should also be in place

to provide a safe framework within which they can explore their new-found independence.

5. **Positive Reinforcement**: Encourage and reward responsible behavior. Recognition often serves as a good motivator for maturity.
6. **Involve Them in Decision Making**: Give them a voice in matters that concern them. This fosters a sense of ownership and accountability.
7. **Prayerful Consideration**: Continually seek God's guidance in your parenting through prayer and consultation of the Scriptures.

Parents who meet the basic physical, emotional, and spiritual needs of their children are laying a strong foundation that can likely prevent rebellion in the adolescent years. These fundamental principles are not just rooted in sound psychology but are deeply biblical, aligning with the whole counsel of God concerning child-rearing.

The Balance of Freedom and Accountability in Adolescent Development

The journey from childhood to adulthood is marked by an increasing sense of freedom and autonomy. However, what often accompanies this newfound freedom is a requirement for greater responsibility and accountability. The Bible unequivocally supports this idea, stating, "whatever a man is sowing, this he will also reap" (Galatians 6:7). Therefore, as parents allow their children greater freedom, they should also hold them accountable for their actions.

Sowing and Reaping: A Biblical Principle

The Bible teaches the law of sowing and reaping, stating that our actions have consequences. This applies to everyone, regardless of age. As children are given more responsibility, they need to be aware of the consequences of their actions. This teaches them to be careful in what they sow because they will reap accordingly. This awareness is an essential part of growing up and becoming responsible adults.

The Importance of Experiencing Consequences

One of the most effective ways to instill the principle of sowing and reaping is to **allow young people to experience the consequences of their decisions and actions**. This does not mean that parents abandon their role as guardians and guides. Instead, it means that they allow natural consequences to take their course when appropriate.

For example, if a teenager neglects their studies, the natural consequence may be a low grade. Instead of stepping in to negotiate with the teacher, the parent may choose to let the child face the result of their actions. This experience serves as a practical lesson, reinforcing the Biblical principle of sowing and reaping.

Setting Boundaries: The Power of "No"

Despite the need for freedom and independence, there are times when parental intervention is necessary, particularly when a child wants to engage in unacceptable activities. In such cases, a firm "No" is not only appropriate but necessary. **Jesus Himself instructs us to let our "yes" be "yes" and our "no" be "no" (Matthew 5:37).** In such instances, while it may be useful to explain the reasons behind the refusal, the decision should not be changed to appease the child.

It's important to note that the manner in which parents say "No" can be just as impactful as the decision itself. Proverbs 15:1 counsels that "an answer, when mild, turns away rage." This suggests that even firm boundaries can be set in a loving, respectful manner that minimizes conflict and emotional turbulence.

As children grow and are given increased responsibility, they should also be taught to face up to the implications of their choices and actions. Balancing freedom with accountability is crucial in helping young people mature into responsible, God-fearing adults. **The**

Biblical principles of sowing and reaping, alongside the need for clear boundaries and godly guidance, provide a robust framework for this important phase of child development.

Addressing the Unique Needs of Teenagers: A Scriptural Guide for Parents

Adolescence is a transformative period marked by significant physical, emotional, and psychological changes. As young people journey through these formative years, it is incumbent upon parents to provide a stable, nurturing environment that aligns with Biblical principles. Below are some key needs that parents should aim to fulfill for their teenagers.

The Need for Consistent Discipline

Scripture emphasizes the importance of discipline in child-rearing. For instance, Proverbs 22:6 states, "Train up a child in the way he should go; even when he is old he will not depart from it." One of the most challenging aspects for teenagers is the inconsistency in rules and boundaries. **Consistency in discipline provides a sense of security**. Frequent changes in rules can be confusing and frustrating for young people, making it difficult for them to understand what is expected of them.

Just as God provides us with steadfast love and clear guidelines, parents should aim to offer a consistent set of rules. This doesn't mean rigidity but rather a stable framework within which the teenager can operate, explore, and grow. *Consistency offers emotional and psychological security, enabling teenagers to navigate the complexities of adolescence more confidently.*

Addressing Emotional Needs: Building Confidence

Adolescence is often a time of vulnerability. Feelings of inadequacy, diffidence, and shyness are common. Isaiah 35:3-4 encourages us to "strengthen the weak hands, and make firm the feeble knees. Say to those who have an anxious heart, 'Be strong; fear not!'"

In line with this Scripture, parents have the role of empowering their teenagers. Offering emotional support and guidance can make a significant difference in how a young person sees themselves and the world around them. By recognizing and addressing these emotional challenges, parents can foster a stronger sense of self-confidence in their teenagers.

Earning and Extending Trust

Trust is a pivotal element in any relationship and is even more crucial during the adolescent years. The Bible praises those who are trustworthy, stating in Luke 16:10, "One who is faithful in a very little is also faithful in much," and again in Luke 19:17, "Well done, good servant! Because you have been faithful in a very little, you shall have authority over ten cities."

Teenagers appreciate it when their efforts to be responsible are acknowledged. Once they demonstrate that they can handle small responsibilities, it's important to entrust them with more. **Recognizing and rewarding trustworthiness encourages maturity and responsibility**.

Being a parent of a teenager is a complex responsibility but also a rewarding one, especially when guided by Biblical principles. By providing consistent discipline, addressing emotional needs, and extending earned trust, parents can significantly contribute to the wholesome development of their teenagers into stable, responsible adults. These are not merely practical tips but fundamental principles rooted deeply in Scripture, aimed at ensuring the well-being of the family in the eyes of God.

Encouraging Truths About Teenagers: A Scriptural Perspective for Hopeful Parents

The teenage years can often be marked by turbulence, not just for the teenagers themselves but also for their parents. However, the Bible offers a multitude of encouraging truths about teenagers that can guide and comfort parents through this challenging phase of parenthood.

The Impact of a Peaceful Home Environment

The Scriptures underscore the importance of maintaining a peaceful and loving household. In Ephesians 4:31-32, Paul admonishes, "Let all bitterness and wrath and anger and clamor and slander be put away from you, along with all malice. Be kind to one another, tenderhearted, forgiving one another, as God in Christ forgave you."

When a home is characterized by these virtues, it serves as fertile ground for the development of stable, mature adults. James 3:17-18 also supports this, saying, "But the wisdom from above is first pure, then peaceable, gentle, open to reason, full of mercy and good fruits, impartial and sincere. And a harvest of righteousness is sown in peace by those who make peace."

In a stable and peaceful home, teenagers are more likely to flourish, even if they have to adhere to reasonable restrictions and discipline. This is in line with God's design for family life.

Resilience in the Face of Adversity

It is encouraging for parents to know that many teenagers have risen above difficult home environments. Some come from families marked by alcoholism, violence, or other harmful influences and still grow up to become responsible, admirable adults. The human spirit, created in the image of God, has a remarkable ability to overcome challenges, especially when fortified by the teachings and principles found in the Bible.

This resilience highlights the innate potential for goodness and growth in every young person, a cause for hope and optimism for all parents. Proverbs 27:11 states, "Be wise, my son, and make my heart glad, that I may answer him who reproaches me."

Security and Love as a Foundation

Ultimately, the most potent ingredients for a successful transition from adolescence to adulthood are *love, affection, and attention*. When teenagers know they are loved and secure, they are more open to guidance and discipline. Providing a secure and loving environment—aligned with Scriptural principles—sets a strong foundation for your child's future.

Parents have the unique opportunity to shape their teenagers into adults they can be proud of. They can leverage this influence by imbibing their homes with the peace, stability, and love that the Bible endorses. In doing so, parents can look forward to a future where their children not only honor them but also honor God.

In summary, the Bible provides a reassuring message for parents of teenagers. Through a stable, loving home environment that's in harmony with Scriptural principles, parents have a significant influence over how their teenagers will grow up. This divine wisdom offers both guidance and hope for families navigating the often turbulent teenage years.

CHAPTER 6 When Children Get Into Difficulty

When Children Get Into Difficulty: Parental Guidance and Children's Accountability

Understanding the dynamics of child-rearing in the light of Scripture requires a balanced approach that takes into account both the responsibilities of the parents and those of the children. While good parenting plays an indispensable role, it's not the only factor in the equation. Let's delve into what the Bible has to say about these nuanced responsibilities.

Parental Responsibility: Training the Child

The Bible offers considerable guidance on the role of parents in shaping their children's character. One of the hallmark passages on this subject is Proverbs 22:6, which states, "Train up a boy according to the way for him; even when he grows old he will not turn aside from it." This passage lays a foundational responsibility upon parents to provide moral, ethical, and spiritual training for their children. The phrase *"according to the way for him"* underscores that this training should be personalized, taking into account the child's unique traits and inclinations.

Good parenting involves more than just laying down rules; it requires teaching children the principles behind those rules, instructing them in the wisdom of God's word so that they can apply it in various circumstances.

The Child's Responsibility: Listening and Obeying

However, as clear as the Bible is about the role of parents, it is equally unambiguous about the responsibilities of the child. In Proverbs 1:8, Scripture urges, "Listen, my son, to your father's instruction and do not forsake your mother's teaching." The onus is not just on the parent to teach but also on the child to listen and obey.

The child, particularly as he or she grows older and moves towards adulthood, has an increasing responsibility to apply the wisdom that has been imparted. Failure to do so could lead to moral, spiritual, and practical pitfalls, creating tension within the family and beyond.

Harmony Through Mutual Responsibility

Both parties—parent and child—must cooperate in applying Scriptural principles to their lives. If only one is doing their part, the Biblical model of family is incomplete, and this incompleteness may lead to difficulties. *It's a cooperative venture between parents and children to ensure that God's principles are followed, resulting in spiritual growth and family harmony.*

When Good Parenting Doesn't Seem to Be Enough

In some instances, children might still get into serious problems despite good parenting. This can be a heartbreaking experience for parents who have done their best to instill solid values and Scriptural principles. It is essential to remember that each individual has free will.

As Ecclesiastes 7:29 reminds us, "See, this alone I found, that God made man upright, but they have sought out many schemes." Even in the best environments, a child might choose a different path. This fact does not absolve the child of responsibility or the consequences of their choices, as emphasized in Galatians 6:7: "Do not be deceived: God is not mocked, for whatever one sows, that will he also reap."

In conclusion, while parents have the primary responsibility to train their children, the children themselves are not passive recipients in this process. They have the responsibility to listen to and act upon the teachings of their parents, as emphasized in Proverbs and other Scriptures. This balance of mutual responsibilities is essential for family harmony and aligns with the overarching Scriptural guidance on family life.

When Children Err Due to Thoughtlessness: A Balanced Approach for Parents

Child-rearing is a journey that involves navigating various emotional terrains, including those tricky moments when a child makes an error due to thoughtlessness. The question at hand is: What would be a wise Scriptural approach for parents when children err in this manner? It's essential to remember that our children, especially teenagers, are in a stage of life marked by a lack of experience and, sometimes, lapses in judgment. Understanding this can help parents respond in a balanced way.

Maintaining a Spirit of Mildness

One guiding principle can be found in Galatians 6:1, which advises, "Even though a man takes some false step before he is aware of it, you who have spiritual qualifications try to readjust such a man in a spirit of mildness." The term *"spirit of mildness"* is critical here. It suggests that parents should approach the erring child not with a punitive spirit but rather with a gentle intent to correct and guide.

Overreacting to the child's mistake can exacerbate the issue and push the child further away, making him or her less likely to listen and learn from the error. Mildness provides an environment where correction is possible, and wisdom can be imparted.

Distinguishing Between the Person and the Action

Jude 22-23 gives further insight, implying that a discerning approach should be applied: "Have mercy on those who doubt; save others by snatching them out of the fire; to others show mercy with fear, hating even the garment stained by the flesh." This suggests that *while the wrong action must be addressed, it should not define the individual*. In dealing with an error made by their child, parents should make it abundantly clear that it is the action that is incorrect, not the child himself or herself.

Providing Constructive Guidance

The goal should always be corrective rather than punitive. The young person needs to understand why the action was wrong and how to avoid it in the future. This is where the role of the parent as a teacher is vital. Proverbs 22:6 advises us to "Train up a child in the way he should go; even when he is old he will not depart from it." In this context, the 'way he should go' includes not just the paths to follow but also how to return to the right path after straying.

Balancing Love and Discipline

Parents must balance love and discipline. Offering love doesn't mean ignoring the error, and providing discipline doesn't mean forgetting love. Ephesians 4:15 encourages us to speak the truth in love, an excellent principle that applies here as well. The child should feel secure in the parents' love even when being corrected, as this fosters a sense of self-worth and openness to growth.

When a child errs due to thoughtlessness, parents would do well to approach the situation with a *spirit of mildness*, focusing on corrective guidance rather than punitive measures. The aim should be to help the child understand the gravity of the error while emphasizing their inherent worth, thus fulfilling the Scriptural principle of raising children in wisdom and love.

Parental Response to a Child's Serious Sin: A Scriptural Approach

In the Christian faith, dealing with sin, especially serious sin, is a matter of great concern and gravity. It calls for tact, wisdom, and above all, spiritual discernment. The question is: How should parents react if their children commit a serious sin, in light of the Scriptural principles and the practices of the Christian church?

Spiritual Restoration Over Concealment

James 5:14-16 says, "Is anyone among you sick? Let him call for the elders of the congregation, and let them pray over him, anointing him with oil in the name of the Lord. And the prayer of faith will save the one who is sick,[1] and the Lord will raise him up. And if he has committed sins, he will be forgiven. Therefore, confess your sins to one another, and pray for one another so that you may be healed. The supplication of a righteous man can accomplish much."

The *first principle* here is the focus on restoration and healing, not merely on judgment or punishment. Similarly, parents should aim for the *spiritual restoration* of their child rather than adopting a punitive approach that could lead to further alienation.

Consultation with Church Pastors

In line with the aforementioned Scriptural passage, when a member of the church sins gravely, they are encouraged to approach the Pastors for spiritual guidance and restoration. Likewise, parents should not hesitate to *seek counsel from the Pastors* when dealing with a child's serious misconduct. *Concealing the sin from the Pastors would be contrary to Scriptural principles* and could endanger both the spiritual well-being of the family and the church.

---

[1] The "sickness" here is a reference to spiritual weakness or sickness, not some physical sickness. The J. P. Lang Commentary says, 1. The calling for the presbyters of the congregation in the Plural; 2. the general direction concerning their prayer accompanying unction with oil; 3. and especially the confident promise that the prayer of faith shall restore the sick, apart from his restoration being connected with the forgiveness of his sins. Was the Apostle warranted to promise bodily recovery in every case in which a sick individual complied with his directions? This misgiving urges us to adopt the symbolical construction of the passage, which would be as follows: if any man as a Christian has been hurt or become sick in his Christianity, let him seek healing from the presbyters, the kernel of the congregation. Let these pray with and for him and anoint him with the oil of the Spirit; such a course wherever taken, will surely restore him and his transgressions will be forgiven him.—John Peter Lange, Philip Schaff, et al., *A Commentary on the Holy Scriptures: James* (Bellingham, WA: Logos Bible Software, 2008), 138.

Parental Responsibility

While it might be tempting for parents to transfer the entire responsibility of their child's spiritual restoration to the Pastors, this would be a mistake. The primary responsibility for helping the erring teenager rests with the parents. Proverbs 22:6 remains relevant here: "Train up a boy according to the way for him; even when he grows old he will not turn aside from it."

Parents are to be the primary spiritual guides for their children, though they should act in harmony with the counsel and recommendations of the Pastors. The focus should always be on what is spiritually best for the child in the eyes of God, even when that involves difficult decisions or actions.

The Goal: Repentance and Restoration

The objective is to bring the erring child to a state of repentance and restoration, just as the Pastors aim to do for erring members of the church. *A key aspect of this is honest, open communication within the family*, grounded in Scriptural principles. Once repentance is observed, the next step is restoration, helping the child to rebuild their spiritual life and regain a healthy relationship with God.

When a child commits a serious sin, parents should not aim for mere punitive measures or concealment. Rather, they should seek the spiritual restoration of their child, acting in concert with the guidance of the Pastors, following the Scriptural model laid out for the church. This approach underscores the importance of mercy, repentance, and spiritual recovery, values deeply embedded in the Christian faith.

Imitating God's Attitude in Parenting: A Scriptural Guide to Handling Serious Errors

Parenting is fraught with challenges and serious errors committed by one's own children could easily be one of the most emotionally draining experiences parents can face. It is in such crucial moments that the need for a Christ-like attitude is most palpable. The Scriptural model provided to us teaches that *attitude is not just a minor detail; it could potentially shape the future of the young soul involved.*

The Temptation to React in Anger

In the heat of the moment, it might be tempting to unleash one's emotional turmoil in the form of anger and threats. But let us consider what Ephesians 4:31 admonishes: "Let all bitterness and wrath and anger and clamor and slander be put away from you, along with all malice." Thus, a reaction fueled by anger not only goes against the Scriptural advice but might also risk *alienating the child further*, making any form of constructive dialogue or repentance difficult.

The Example of God's Forgiveness

Isaiah 1:18 provides a sterling example of the kind of attitude parents should adopt. It says, "'Come now, let us set matters straight,' says Jehovah: 'though your sins are like scarlet, they will be made as white as snow; though they are red like crimson, they will become like wool.'"

Jehovah is willing to forgive, even grievous sins, if there is repentance. This shows *God's propensity for mercy and readiness to restore a broken relationship* rather than discard it. This is the attitude that parents should aim to imitate.

The Importance of a Balanced Approach

While it's essential to correct the error, it is equally important to make the child understand that while the action is condemned, they as individuals are not. The focus should be on helping them see the gravity of their mistake and leading them to repentance, rather than shaming or embittering them. This will be more likely to bring about a genuine change of heart, in keeping with the Scriptural principle found in 2 Corinthians 7:10: "For godly grief produces a repentance that leads to salvation without regret, whereas worldly grief produces death."

The Critical Nature of This Juncture

The child's future may very well hinge on how they are treated during this period of error. A punitive approach might produce a child who learns to hide errors better, while a permissive approach may yield a child who doesn't appreciate the gravity of sin. However, an approach that combines love with righteous standards, *as God exemplifies*, has the power to produce a repentant and spiritually robust child.

In conclusion, when dealing with a child who has committed a serious error, parents should strive to imitate God's balance of justice and mercy. This approach respects the gravity of the sin while leaving room for repentance and restoration, just as God has done countless times with His own people.

Navigating the Difficult Terrain: Parental Approach to a Child's Serious Sin

Confronting the stark reality that your child has committed a serious sin can be emotionally wrenching. Yet, the Scriptures provide a balanced and comprehensive guide for parents dealing with such difficult circumstances. The underlying thread of the biblical message is *a call to wisdom, temperance, and undying love*—traits that must inform every action and decision in these challenging times.

The Importance of Wisdom and Sound Advice

Solomon penned, "Where there is no guidance, a people falls, but in an abundance of counselors there is safety" (Proverbs 11:14). The first step for parents should be to seek counsel from experienced parents and congregation elders. This advice serves to offer perspective, practical insights, and importantly, emotional stability. *Impulsive decisions are almost always regrettable and could erect barriers that make the child's return to righteousness more challenging.*

Guarding Against Uncontrolled Emotions

Colossians 3:8 admonishes, "But now you must put them all away: anger, wrath, malice, slander, and obscene talk from your mouth." Emotions are heightened in the face of a child's grave sin, yet this is the time when parents must demonstrate a Christ-like mastery over their feelings. *Impulsive words or actions could irrevocably damage the relationship and make it difficult for the child to seek repentance.*

The Virtue of Perseverance

One of the most testing aspects of parenting is not giving up on a child who seems to be persistently wayward. Scripture encourages us to love continually. 1 Corinthians 13:4, 7 tells us that love "bears all things, believes all things, hopes all things, endures all things." The resilience to stay the course, guided by Christian love, can often make the difference between a child who strays permanently and one who finds his way back. *Enduring love may well be the anchor that draws the wayward child back to the fold.*

Balancing Abhorrence for Sin with Love for the Child

While the Scriptures are clear about hating what is bad, they also caution against becoming hard and embittered, particularly toward someone you have nurtured and loved. Parents must make it clear that it is the sin they despise, not the child. This distinction not only follows Christ's example but can also open the door to genuine repentance and reconciliation.

Keeping the Faith and Setting the Example

Lastly, but most significantly, maintaining strong faith in God is crucial. A parent's steadfastness and righteous example often serve as a silent yet powerful sermon for their children. The Apostle Paul reminds us in 1 Timothy 4:12 to "set the believers an example in speech, in conduct, in love, in faith, in purity."

In conclusion, the path of parenting through a child's serious sin is fraught with emotional and spiritual pitfalls. Yet, armed with Scriptural wisdom, a controlled demeanor, and an unwavering commitment to love and faith, parents can provide a secure bridge for a wayward child to cross back into the fold.

CHAPTER 7 Handling a Determined Rebel

The Heartbreaking Reality: Dealing with a Determined Rebel in a Christian Home

It is indeed a grievous situation when, despite the best efforts, a child chooses the path of persistent rebellion, rejecting the Christian values instilled in the home. These are situations that wrench the heart and stir the soul, as they carry not just temporal but eternal consequences. Yet even in such trials, *Scripture offers guidance, wisdom, and, importantly, hope.*

Reorienting the Family Focus

In instances where rebellion is definitive and Christian values are outright rejected by a youth, Proverbs 20:18 advises, "Plans are established by seeking advice; so if you wage war, obtain guidance." The "war" here is, of course, a spiritual one, and the advice should be geared toward preserving the faith and integrity of those still committed to Christian values within the family. *The focus should shift from expending all emotional and spiritual energy on the rebellious child to maintaining or rebuilding the spiritual health of the remaining family members.*

The Necessity of Balanced Attention

It's easy to get consumed by the actions of the rebellious child, allowing their choices to overshadow the needs of other children who are walking faithfully. This lack of balance could unintentionally lead to other family members feeling neglected or even tempted to stray, thinking that it's the only way to receive attention. Parents must ensure they are not directing all their energy and resources to the rebel at the expense of the rest of the family.

Openness and Communication within the Family

While there may be a natural inclination to shield the other children from the full extent of the issue, *it's essential to discuss the matter openly, yet carefully.* This does not mean divulging every sordid detail, but rather communicating the general situation and how the family plans to cope. Honest, age-appropriate conversations about the rebellion can help the remaining children understand the serious implications of straying from the path of righteousness, while also ensuring that they do not feel left in the dark or burdened by a "family secret."

A Note of Caution

The course of wisdom in dealing with a determined rebel does not mean that parents emotionally or spiritually abandon the erring child. Rather, they assume a stance similar to that of the father of the Prodigal Son—always hopeful for repentance and ready to forgive (Luke 15:11-32). But *this hope does not preclude the necessary adjustments within the family to preserve its overall spiritual health.*

The challenges posed by a determined rebel in a Christian family require *wisdom, spiritual balance, and open communication.* While the situation is undoubtedly painful, sticking closely to Scriptural principles can provide a sturdy ship to navigate these tumultuous waters.

A Most Difficult Challenge: Addressing a Determined Rebel within a Christian Household

The issue of dealing with a rebellious child who reaches a point of being a determined rebel is among the most heart-wrenching challenges a Christian parent can face. *How far should discipline go? What actions may be necessary to safeguard the spiritual welfare of the household?* These questions require the utmost care, prayer, and above all, wisdom from the Scriptures.

The Extreme Measure: Disassociation with a Rebellious Child

In 2 John 10, we read a severe directive from the Apostle John regarding how to deal with someone who deviates significantly from the teachings of Christ: "Never receive him into your homes or say a greeting to him." This Scriptural principle may serve as a guideline for parents dealing with a child of legal age who becomes a determined rebel. **Though exceedingly difficult, it may become necessary to remove the rebellious child from the family setting.** This step is not taken lightly and is considered only after all other avenues have been exhausted. The aim is to protect the spiritual welfare of other family members.

The Protection of the Family: Clearly Defined Boundaries

It's crucial to *maintain clearly defined, yet reasonable, boundaries* within the family. These boundaries are not just rules for the sake of rules but are guided by Scriptural principles designed to cultivate righteousness and godly devotion. "Train up a child in the way he should go; even when he is old he will not depart from it" (Proverbs 22:6). Your remaining children need your ongoing oversight, not merely to adhere to a set of regulations but to understand and appreciate the principles underlying them.

Open Communication: The Emotional and Spiritual Pulse of the Family

You should maintain open lines of communication with the other children. Be invested in their academic and spiritual lives, noting how they are progressing in school and in their roles within the congregation. This focused attention serves to show that your concerns extend beyond mere rule enforcement to their overall well-being.

Differentiating Between the Child and Their Actions

The importance of condemning the action rather than the child cannot be overstated. *Make it clear that you do not hate the rebellious child but disapprove of his or her actions.* The Bible itself sets the precedent for this in the case of Jacob and his sons Simeon and Levi in Genesis 34:1-31 and 49:5-7. When they committed a violent act against the Shechemites, Jacob condemned their violent anger but did not disown his sons. In his dying blessings, he voiced strong disapproval of their actions, delineating between the person and the sin.

The Biblical Balance: Love, Discipline, and Wisdom

In summary, the parent's role in confronting a determined rebel within the family framework must be navigated with *deep love, Scriptural discipline, and divinely inspired wisdom.* All actions should aim for the repentance and spiritual restoration of the rebellious child, but not to the detriment of the spiritual health of the rest of the family. These are painful choices to make, but as stewards of our households, our primary allegiance is to uphold the sanctity and righteousness that God expects.

Finding Comfort Amidst the Rebellion of a Child: A Spiritual Perspective for Conscientious Parents

Handling rebellion in a child can be emotionally devastating, leaving you questioning your effectiveness as a parent. You may feel crushed by guilt or think that you've failed as a parent. However, in such trying times, conscientious parents can find comfort in several crucial principles derived from Scripture.

You're Not Alone: God Understands

It's essential to recognize that you are not navigating these turbulent waters alone. God understands the human condition and the complexities of parenting. *Psalm 27:10 reminds us that even if our father and mother abandon us, Jehovah will take us in.* God's loving-kindness doesn't waver, even when you face insurmountable challenges with a rebellious child.

Limitations of Human Efforts: Imperfection and Free Will

No parent is perfect. Every parent makes mistakes, even those who diligently strive to follow God's counsel. In Acts 20:26, Paul clears his conscience before God and men, declaring that he is innocent of anyone's blood because he did not hesitate to preach the whole purpose of God. Like Paul, if you have prayerfully done your best to impart Christian values and wisdom to your child, your conscience can be clear before God.

Remember, children, especially as they age, exert their free will, sometimes in opposition to what they've been taught. *Your child's decision to rebel is not a direct reflection of your worth or effectiveness as a parent.* You are responsible for providing the right guidance, but ultimately, each individual has to make their own choices.

Preserving Spiritual Integrity in the Remaining Family

The rebellion of one child should not derail your commitment to maintaining a spiritually healthy home environment for your other children. Continue to build your home into a sanctuary of spiritual values and ethical living. This is where the rest of the family can find comfort, safety, and spiritual nourishment. By doing so, you not only preserve the spiritual integrity of the home but also offer a godly model for your remaining children to follow.

The Comfort of a Good Conscience and Unwavering Faith

While you may not be able to control the choices that your adult children make, you do have control over your own integrity and devotion to God. You've done your best, and God sees that. Therefore, lean on your unwavering faith and a good conscience to find comfort during these heart-wrenching times.

The rebellion of a child is undeniably painful and disheartening, but it doesn't have to define you as a parent or as a servant of God. By leaning on Scriptural principles and sustaining an unwavering faith in God, you can find comfort and continue to serve as a spiritual pillar for the rest of your family.

The Hope of Restoration: Insights from the Parable of the Prodigal Son

The emotional strain experienced by parents of a rebellious child can be overwhelming. However, within the Scriptures, there are seeds of hope that can comfort distressed parents. The parable of the prodigal son, recorded in Luke 15:11-32, is one such oasis of hope.

The Eternal Power of Early Training

One of the most heartening elements to consider is the role of early training in a child's life. *Ecclesiastes 11:6 advises us to "sow your seed in the morning, and at evening let your hands not be idle, for you do not know which will succeed, whether this or that, or whether both will do equally well."* This is a timeless principle applicable to child-rearing. The seeds you've sown in your child's heart through years of prayerful guidance may lie dormant for a time but can potentially sprout and bring forth good fruit.

The Unpredictable Yet Possible Return

The story of the prodigal son is essentially one of rebellion, repentance, and restoration. The son in the parable strayed far from his father's home, wasting his inheritance in reckless living. But a time of crisis led him to "come to his senses" and return home, where he was met not with punishment but with a loving embrace and a celebratory feast.

You too can hold onto the hope that your child may come to a point of realization, repenting and returning to the values you've instilled. It might take an event of significant impact, or it could be a gradual process. The important takeaway is that *rebellion is not always the final chapter in a child's life.*

Lessons from Christian Families and the Scriptures

It's not just a parable; many Christian families have lived through this painful experience. Some have seen their children stray far from their Christian upbringing, only to return after years, much like the prodigal son. Your family may witness a similar restoration. Such instances stand as testament to the enduring power of proper training and the grace of Jehovah.

The Vital Importance of Hope

As you navigate this painful period, maintaining hope is not just an option but a necessity. Hope based on Scriptural principles and the reality of human changeability can serve as an anchor. It sustains you emotionally and spiritually and allows you to be prepared should your child choose to return to the teachings they received early in life.

In conclusion, the parable of the prodigal son and the wisdom literature in the Bible offer parents much-needed hope. Your labors in teaching your child the ways of God are not in vain, even if their effects are not immediately visible. Continue to place your trust in God's principles and never relinquish the hope that your wayward child might one day return, humbled and repentant, just like the prodigal son.

CHAPTER 8 Bible Principles that Can Help Parents Prevent Serious Rebellion

Preventing Serious Rebellion in the Household: Guided by Scripture

The home is meant to be a sanctuary from the world, a place where Christian values reign and the spirit of God is felt. Yet, the threat of rebellion always lurks, especially as children grow and are exposed to external influences. This makes the parent's role crucial in safeguarding the household from serious rebellion. Here are Bible principles that can aid parents in this endeavor.

The Power of Association: Learning from Proverbs 13:20

Proverbs 13:20 tells us, "He who walks with wise men will be wise, but the companion of fools will be broken." This is a foundational principle that parents must internalize. Children, especially during their teenage years, are highly susceptible to the influence of their peer group. Parents need to be vigilant about who their children associate with. Encourage friendships within the faith, and be wary of worldly associations that could lead your child down a path of rebellion.

The World's Spirit: Caution from Ephesians 2:2

Ephesians 2:2 refers to "*the prince of the power of the air, the spirit that is now at work in the sons of disobedience.*" This is a stark reminder that there are spiritual forces at work aiming to corrupt the young. This isn't just a matter of peer influence; it's a battle for the spiritual well-being of your child. Parents need to instill in their children a strong sense of discernment so that they can recognize and resist the "world's spirit."

Practical Steps Rooted in Scripture

1. **Open Lines of Communication**: Parents should establish a safe space for open dialogue about faith, friendships, and any challenges the child might be facing. *James 1:19 advises us to be "quick to hear, slow to speak, slow to anger."*
2. **Regular Family Worship**: Establish a routine of family worship and Bible study. *Deuteronomy 6:6-7 emphasizes the need to teach the words of Jehovah diligently to your children, discussing them at home and on the way.*
3. **Active Participation in Church Activities**: Being part of a spiritual community can serve as an additional layer of protection against worldly influences. *Hebrews 10:24-25 exhorts us not to forsake the gathering of ourselves.*
4. **Modelling Christian Living**: The best way to teach is often to show. Parents need to model Christian virtues in their everyday lives. *Titus 2:7-8 talks about showing yourself in all respects to be a model of good works.*

Trusting in God's Guidance

All of these steps should be carried out with constant prayer for wisdom and guidance from God. *Philippians 4:6-7 encourages us to make our requests known to God through prayer and thanksgiving.*

In conclusion, while it may seem like a daunting task to shield your household from rebellion in a world filled with corrupting influences, the Bible provides sound guidance for this endeavor. Parents who diligently apply Scriptural principles can build a home that stands as a bulwark against the spirit of the world, thereby preventing serious rebellion within their household.

Striking a Balance: The Antidote to Household Rebellion

One of the most significant challenges facing Christian parents today is managing the delicate balance between being too restrictive and too permissive in their parenting approach. This balance is crucial in preventing serious rebellion within the household. Scripture offers profound wisdom for parents who are grappling with this challenge.

The Danger of Excessive Restrictiveness: Insight from Ecclesiastes 7:7

The Bible cautions, *"Surely oppression drives the wise into madness, and a bribe corrupts the heart."* (Ecclesiastes 7:7, UASV) When children feel oppressed by overly strict rules or an authoritarian environment, it can drive them toward rebellion. Over-restrictiveness often stifles a child's personal growth and can incite a counter-reaction.

Parents must be careful to not create an atmosphere of "oppression," where their wisdom may turn into what is perceived as madness by the youth. A balanced approach would involve setting necessary boundaries while giving the child room to grow, make mistakes, and learn from them.

The Risk of Too Much Permissiveness: Learning from Ecclesiastes 8:11

Ecclesiastes 8:11 warns, *"Because the sentence against an evil deed is not executed quickly, the heart of the sons of man is fully set to do evil."* When there are no boundaries or consequences for actions, it paves the way for increased disobedience and rebellion. Permissiveness sends the message that rules and guidelines are flexible, leading the child to think that they can get away with inappropriate behavior.

When children do not face timely consequences for their actions, their hearts may become "fully set to do evil." A lack of discipline could be misconstrued as tacit approval of wrongdoing, thereby emboldening a rebellious spirit.

Achieving a Balanced Approach: Practical Steps

1. **Defined Boundaries, Not High Walls**: Create boundaries that protect but do not smother. *Proverbs 22:6 says, "Train up a child in the way he should go; even when he is old he will not depart from it."*

2. **Consistent but Compassionate Discipline**: Apply disciplinary measures that are consistent but laced with understanding and love. *Ephesians 6:4 advises fathers not to provoke their children to anger but bring them up in the discipline and instruction of the Lord.*

3. **Engage in Open Dialogue**: Freely discuss the reasons behind family rules, incorporating the child's viewpoint when reasonable. *James 1:19 reminds us to be "quick to listen, slow to speak, slow to anger."*

4. **Be a Model, Not a Dictator**: Demonstrate through your own actions how to live a godly life. *1 Corinthians 11:1 says, "Be imitators of me, as I am of Christ."*

Divine Support in a Balanced Approach

Maintaining this balance can be challenging, but God provides wisdom and guidance for those who seek it. *James 1:5 says, "If any of you lacks wisdom, let him ask God, who gives generously to all without reproach, and it will be given him."*

By striking the correct balance between restrictiveness and permissiveness, parents can create an environment where rebellion is less likely to take root. This balanced approach, supported by Scriptural principles, allows parents to guide their children on the path of righteousness without pushing them towards the perils of rebellion.

Addressing Wrong Conduct with Mildness: A Strategy for Rebellion Prevention

Christian parents are often faced with the crucial task of addressing wrong conduct in their children, and the manner in which they deal with such matters can significantly affect the likelihood of rebellion within the household. It is imperative that corrective action aligns with Scriptural principles. One such important principle is found in Galatians 6:1: *"Brothers, even if a man is caught in some transgression, you who are spiritual should restore such a one in a spirit of mildness, keeping an eye on yourself, so that you also will not be tempted."* Let us dive into this key text and its implications for parenting.

The Imperative of Mildness: A Closer Look at Galatians 6:1

The apostle Paul is explicit about the need for a *spirit of mildness* when dealing with transgressions. The word "mildness" here is critical. It implies that the corrective action should be free from harshness, severity, or undue anger. The objective is not punitive but restorative, aiming to bring the individual back into a proper relationship with God and the family.

Risks of Approaching Wrong Conduct Without Mildness

Handling a child's misconduct with an authoritarian or overly punitive approach may incite further rebellion and estrangement. Such a course could result in alienating the child and leading them further away from God, negating the purpose of discipline, which is to restore the individual to a godly path.

Practical Steps to Implement Mildness

1. **Take Time to Calm Down**: *Proverbs 14:29 says, "Whoever is slow to anger has great understanding, but he who has a hasty temper exalts folly."* Before addressing the wrong conduct, give yourself time to calm down and think rationally about the situation.

2. **Consult Scripture for Guidance**: Meditate on relevant Scriptures that can inform your approach. *Psalm 119:105 describes God's word as "a lamp to my feet and a light to my path."*

3. **Open Dialogue**: Instead of issuing decrees, engage your child in a conversation, allowing them to express their feelings and understand the gravity of their actions. *James 1:19 advises, "Know this, my beloved brothers: let every person be quick to hear, slow to speak, slow to anger."*

4. **Clarify the Spiritual Implications**: Make sure the child understands how the wrong conduct is not just against family rules but also against God's standards. *Colossians 3:20 advises children to "obey your parents in everything, for this pleases the Lord."*

5. **Establish Restorative Measures**: Rather than simply punishing the child, focus on measures that can restore them spiritually and morally. This could include increased Bible study, prayer, or involvement in wholesome activities.

The Blessings of Mildness

A mild approach is likely to be more effective in preventing serious rebellion. It helps the child feel loved and understood, even while correcting them. This fosters an environment where the child feels safe to grow spiritually and morally, reducing the likelihood of rebellion.

In summary, dealing with wrong conduct in a spirit of mildness is not just a nice suggestion; it is a Scriptural mandate for parents who aim to prevent serious rebellion in their household. This approach ensures that discipline is balanced, fair, and ultimately, redemptive.

Edward D. Andrews

CHAPTER 9 Help Your Teenager to Thrive

Navigating the Challenges and Joys of the Teen Years: A Biblical Perspective

Parenting teenagers is a unique chapter in the lifelong journey of raising children. This period is often marked by a mix of challenges and joys. While the Scriptures don't explicitly use the term "teenagers," we find examples of young individuals like Joseph, David, Josiah, and Timothy who navigated the complexities of youth in a way that pleased Jehovah. Their stories, along with principles found in the Word of God, can provide valuable insights for parents and teenagers alike.

Biblical Examples of Responsible Youth

1. **Joseph**: At 17, Joseph exhibited maturity and responsibility in his duties. His father, Jacob, trusted him enough to report on his brothers' activities (Genesis 37:2-11).

2. **David**: Still a youth when he faced Goliath, David demonstrated faith and courage beyond his years (1 Samuel 16:11-13).

3. **Josiah**: Became king at a young age and led one of the most significant religious reforms in Israel's history (2 Kings 22:3-7).

4. **Timothy**: Timothy was well-spoken of by his community and was a trusted companion of the Apostle Paul (Acts 16:1-2).

These examples show that young people *can act responsibly and have a fine relationship with Jehovah.*

Challenges of the Teen Years

1. **Emotional Volatility**: Adolescents often experience emotional ups and downs due to hormonal changes and the struggles of finding their identity.
2. **Desire for Independence**: Teenagers may seek more freedom, sometimes chafing against parental guidelines and oversight.
3. **Inexperience**: Despite a craving for independence, adolescents are relatively inexperienced in life, making them vulnerable to mistakes and poor judgment.
4. **Conflict with Parents**: As teens push for autonomy, they may resent limits imposed by their parents, leading to potential tension within the family.

Joys of the Teen Years

1. **Emerging Maturity**: One of the delights of this stage is seeing your child grow in responsibility and make wise choices.
2. **Deepening Relationship with God**: Teens like Josiah and Timothy can develop a profound relationship with God, which can be immensely satisfying for a Christian parent to witness.
3. **Individual Talents**: This is often the time when unique gifts and talents begin to surface, which can be a source of joy and pride.
4. **Preparation for Adulthood**: The teen years can be a fulfilling period of preparation for adult responsibilities and privileges, including involvement in the work of the Kingdom.

Guiding Youth Through These Pivotal Years

1. **Foster Open Communication**: *James 1:19 advises, "Know this, my beloved brothers: let every person be quick to hear, slow to speak, slow*

to anger." Effective communication helps to understand your teen's challenges and aspirations.

2. **Provide Balanced Limits:** As Ecclesiastes 7:7 suggests, *extortion turns a wise person into a fool, and a bribe corrupts the heart.* Limits should be neither too permissive nor too restrictive to avoid driving teens to rebellion or compromise.
3. **Encourage Spiritual Growth:** Personal and family study, prayer, and participation in Christian meetings can fortify their relationship with God. *Psalm 119:105 says, "Your word is a lamp to my feet and a light to my path."*
4. **Model Christian Virtues:** Teens are more likely to emulate what they see. Make sure your conduct sets a positive example (1 Corinthians 11:1).

While the teen years can be both challenging and rewarding, a balanced, Scripturally grounded approach can help parents and teenagers navigate this period successfully, in a way that is pleasing to God.

Providing Adolescents with a Fine Opportunity in Life: A Scriptural Guide for Parents

The teen years are a pivotal phase, often filled with various trials and challenges. However, it's also an incredibly formative period where values are solidified, character is shaped, and the foundation for future adulthood is laid. According to Scripture, parents have a divine mandate and incredible opportunity to shepherd their adolescent children through these crucial years. So how can parents offer the best possible opportunity for their teens to successfully navigate through the trials of adolescence into responsible adulthood?

Adherence to Biblical Principles: The Time-Tested Pathway to Success

It is unambiguously stated in *Psalm 119:1, "Blessed are those whose way is blameless, who walk in the law of the Lord!"* When parents and teenagers jointly adhere to the biblical standards, they are setting themselves up for success. This is not a modern phenomenon; it has been proven time and again, across cultures and throughout history. Therefore, adherence to biblical counsel gives teenagers the unparalleled advantage of divine wisdom and principles, which far surpass human reasoning.

Instilling a Love for God's Word

Inculcating a deep-rooted respect and love for Scripture in adolescents sets them up for a lifelong relationship with Jehovah. *Deuteronomy 6:6-7 advises, "And these words that I command you today shall be on your heart. You shall teach them diligently to your children, and shall talk of them when you sit in your house, and when you walk by the way, and when you lie down, and when you rise."* The home should be a haven where God's Word is esteemed and discussed regularly.

Providing a Safe and Spiritual Environment

According to *Psalm 27:10, "For my father and my mother have forsaken me, but the Lord will take me in."* Even when adolescents stray, a home grounded in biblical principles serves as a spiritual sanctuary. Parents need to keep the spiritual atmosphere of the home alive, ensuring it remains a place of refuge and peace based on the wisdom found in God's Word.

Emphasizing Moral and Ethical Training

Values like integrity, honesty, humility, and kindness need to be taught explicitly and caught implicitly. *Proverbs 22:6 instructs, "Train up a child in the way he should go; even when he is old he will not depart from it."* Adolescents, with their still-forming moral compass, would do well to have parents who not only speak about these virtues but also model them.

Encouragement and Positive Reinforcement

Building an adolescent's self-esteem and confidence through biblical encouragement can make a world of difference. Scripture offers countless examples and principles that parents can use to build their teens up. *1 Thessalonians 5:11 tells us, "Therefore encourage one another and build one another up, just as you are doing."*

Fostering Responsibility and Work Ethic

Teaching an adolescent the value of responsibility and a strong work ethic aligns with biblical principles. *Colossians 3:23 states, "Whatever you do, work heartily, as for the Lord and not for men."* In doing so, parents provide their adolescent offspring the tools they need to be responsible adults.

Prayerful Dependence on God

Last but certainly not least, a reliance on prayer is critical. *James 5:16 assures us, "The prayer of a righteous person has great power as it is working."* Consistent, heartfelt prayers for your adolescent children not only invite divine intervention but also demonstrate to them the importance of a personal relationship with God.

Parents who diligently apply Scriptural principles in the upbringing of their adolescent children are giving them the finest opportunity to navigate the complexities of this life stage successfully. By doing so, they lay a strong foundation for their children's eventual transition into responsible, God-fearing adults.

CHAPTER 10 Honest and Open Communication

The Imperative of Honest and Open Communication During the Teen Years

The teen years are a formative period, characterized by a search for independence, identity, and deeper emotional and intellectual understanding. It's a stage where adolescents begin to navigate complex relationships outside the home. As they face these new challenges, the need for honest and open communication with parents becomes paramount. The Bible reminds us, *"There is a frustrating of plans where there is no confidential talk"* (Proverbs 15:22). This Scriptural principle is particularly relevant to families with teenagers.

The Necessity of Confidential Talk in a Biblical Context

The importance of confidential talk is highlighted in the wisdom literature of Scripture, specifically in *Proverbs 15:22*. The verse cautions against the lack of consultation or secretive behavior as it leads to the "frustrating of plans." In a household setting, this principle is critically important. If confidential talk is necessary during childhood, it becomes doubly vital during the adolescent years when the stakes are higher and the challenges are more complex.

The Risk of Emotional Estrangement

One of the gravest risks of poor communication during the teen years is the emotional estrangement that may develop between parents and teens. Without open channels of communication, the parent-child relationship can become superficial, restricted to surface-level interactions. *Proverbs 18:1* warns, *"Whoever isolates himself seeks his own desire; he breaks out against all sound judgment."* The absence of confidential talk can make teenagers "strangers in the house," vulnerable to poor judgment and external influences that are not in line with Christian principles.

Facilitating Open Communication Channels

So how can the lines of communication be kept open?

Active Listening

Active listening is crucial. Parents should cultivate an environment where teens feel comfortable expressing their thoughts and feelings. *James 1:19 advises, "Know this, my beloved brothers: let every person be quick to hear, slow to speak, slow to anger."*

Non-Judgmental Approach

Parents should aim to be non-judgmental and receptive to their teen's perspective. *Colossians 3:21 cautions, "Fathers, do not provoke your children, lest they become discouraged."* A harsh or judgmental tone can shut down communication, making confidential talk nearly impossible.

Scheduled Family Time

Designated family times can provide a structured environment for deep conversations. *Deuteronomy 6:7 suggests, "You shall teach them diligently to your children, and shall talk of them when you sit in your house, and when you walk by the way, and when you lie down, and when you rise."*

Encouragement and Affirmation

Encouragement and affirmation should be liberally dispensed to bolster the child's confidence in discussing matters openly. *1 Thessalonians 5:11 states, "Therefore encourage one another and build one another up, just as you are doing."*

Scriptural Guidance

Above all, conversations should be anchored in Scriptural guidance. *Psalm 119:105 declares, "Your word is a lamp to my feet and a light to my path."* Introducing biblical principles during confidential talks can serve as both a moral compass and a source of comfort.

The teen years are a critical period that demands heightened confidential talk between parents and children. Such honest and open communication aligns with biblical wisdom, serves to guide the adolescent through challenging times, and fortifies the emotional and spiritual bonds within the Christian household.

The Mutual Responsibility in Communication: A Biblical Guide for Teenagers

While much emphasis is placed on the role parents play in facilitating open communication, it's crucial to recognize that teenagers also have a vital role in this dynamic. Indeed, the teen years present their own unique challenges and complexities that make open dialogue more essential yet potentially more strained. However, the Bible offers wisdom in this regard, stating, *"when there is no skillful direction, the people fall; but there is salvation in the multitude of counselors"* (Proverbs 11:14).

The Weight of Proverbs 11:14 in the Teen Context

The wisdom from *Proverbs 11:14* holds true for both parents and teenagers. This verse underscores the importance of counsel and guidance. For teenagers, this is an especially pertinent lesson. Adolescence is a time of great change and new experiences, often including challenges that may be more complex than those faced during earlier years. This is precisely why the word of God emphasizes the "multitude of counselors." As adolescents navigate these complex issues, they still need "skillful direction," which can come from experienced and godly counselors.

Recognizing Parents as Qualified Counselors

One of the significant steps for teenagers is to acknowledge their parents as a primary source of this "skillful direction." Parents, particularly those who follow the counsel of Scripture, are uniquely qualified to offer this guidance. Their years of life experience, coupled with their proven loving concern, make them invaluable resources for advice and emotional support.

A Testament to Time and Love

It is essential to appreciate that parents have "proved their loving concern over many years." Their counsel is not just theoretical but is backed by practical experience and a deeply vested interest in their children's well-being. Moreover, their advice aligns with Biblical values, offering teenagers a moral compass during challenging times.

Why Wise Teenagers Will Not Turn Away

Adolescents need to confront the notion that declaring independence doesn't mean severing important emotional and spiritual lifelines. *Ephesians 6:1-3 says, "Children, obey your parents in the Lord, for this is right. 'Honor your father and mother' (this is the first commandment with a promise), 'that it may go well with you and that you may live long in the land.'"* There is a promise attached to honoring and listening to parents. In doing so, teenagers are not just complying with a Biblical command; they are also setting the stage for their well-being.

Complex Issues Demand Experienced Counsel

As the issues teenagers face become more complex, ranging from emotional to ethical dilemmas, the counsel of parents becomes invaluable. *Psalm 1:1 states, "Blessed is the man who walks not in the counsel of the wicked, nor stands in the way of sinners, nor sits in the seat of scoffers."* In a world where ungodly counsel is readily available, particularly through social media and peer pressure, the godly counsel of believing parents serves as a protective and guiding force.

The Bible instructs that wisdom can often be found in the counsel of the experienced. For teenagers, this should mean recognizing the invaluable resource they have in their parents. The challenges of the adolescent years make the wisdom and counsel of parents not less, but more critical. Wise teenagers, understanding the Biblical imperatives and practicalities, will not turn away from this godly source of skillful direction.

The Role of Parents in Fostering Open Communication: A Biblical Perspective

Navigating the turbulent waters of adolescent emotional development and autonomy can be a complicated process. While adolescents bear a certain responsibility for maintaining open lines of communication, parents have an equally significant, if not more crucial, role to play. Scripture provides ample guidance on the attitude that wise and loving parents should adopt when it comes to conversing with their teenage children.

The Importance of Availability: Learning from Ecclesiastes 3:7

The Bible reminds us that there is "*a time to keep quiet and a time to speak*" (Ecclesiastes 3:7). Parents must have the wisdom to discern the appropriate moments for each. When a teenager feels the need to talk, that becomes the parent's "time to speak," or more accurately, a time to listen.

Open communication means that the parent will try hard to be available when the teenager feels the need to talk. This may require making sacrifices in terms of personal time, be it for relaxation, study, or household chores. The key here is willingness and flexibility. Parents need to be open to adjusting their plans for the sake of their children's emotional and spiritual well-being.

The Christlike Example: A Lesson from Mark 6:30-34

Consider the life of Jesus Christ as an exemplary model. In Mark 6:30-34, Jesus had planned some time to relax. Yet, when people crowded around Him, eager for spiritual nourishment, He set aside His own needs to cater to theirs. While the context is different, the principle holds value for parents. *If your child needs to talk, be prepared to put aside your immediate concerns to listen, just as Jesus did.* The message this sends to the teenager is profoundly impactful: "You matter, your concerns are valid, and I am here for you."

The Emotional and Psychological Benefits of Availability

Most teenagers are acutely aware that their parents lead busy lives. However, they need the reassurance that, despite these responsibilities, their parents are available and understanding. This is not merely a logistical issue but a deeply emotional and psychological one. Adolescents often find themselves in a confusing landscape of social pressures and emotional upheavals. Knowing that they have a safe, non-judgmental space in their parents can be a powerful stabilizing force.

Practicing Active Listening: Beyond Mere Availability

Being available is only the first step; parents must also engage in active listening. This involves not just hearing the words but seeking to understand the emotions and thoughts behind them. *Proverbs 18:2 states, "A fool takes no pleasure in understanding, but only in expressing his opinion."* The objective here is not to formulate an immediate response or solution but to genuinely understand the teenager's perspective. Parents must realize that the act of listening itself can be an incredibly validating experience for a teenager, which can fortify emotional bonds.

Be Available, Be Understanding

Open communication is a two-way street. However, the onus is largely on parents to set the stage for this to happen effectively. Taking cues from Scripture, wise and loving parents will make themselves available and adaptable to their teenager's needs, just as Jesus was to the crowds that sought His wisdom. By embodying these virtues, parents not only facilitate open dialogue but also exemplify Christlike love and understanding, fortifying their family's spiritual foundation.

Potential Pitfalls Parents Must Avoid: A Scriptural Guide to Nurturing Adolescent Relationships

As parents navigate the complex emotional terrain that comes with raising teenagers, there are specific pitfalls they need to avoid to ensure a healthy familial relationship. These traps are often subtle and may escape immediate notice, but their long-term impact can be profoundly damaging.

The Danger of Emotional Distancing: An Overlooked Problem

When there is free time available, how do the parents spend it? Parents may inadvertently create emotional distancing by how they allocate their leisure time. If parents consistently use their free time to engage in activities that don't include their family, this can send an unintended message. It may cause adolescents to feel emotionally marginalized and lead them to think that they are not a priority in their parents' lives. The consequences can be severe. *If adolescents conclude that school friends value them more than their own parents, this perception will cause significant problems.*

The Importance of Quality Time: Wisdom from Deuteronomy 6:6-7

This issue of time allocation ties back to Scriptural principles. Deuteronomy 6:6-7 says, "And these words that I command you today shall be on your heart. You shall teach them diligently to your children, and shall talk of them when you sit in your house, and when you walk by the way, and when you lie down, and when you rise." This Scripture emphasizes the importance of quality time spent in spiritual and emotional nourishment. There is an implied inclusivity in family activities, underlined by the multiple settings in which teaching and communication are encouraged.

Retaining a Sense of Humor and Empathy: Learning from Proverbs 17:22

Try to remember what it was like when you were a teenager, and do not lose your sense of humor! Proverbs 17:22 instructs, "A cheerful heart is good medicine, but a crushed spirit dries up the bones." Humor is not just an emotional relief but can be a relational glue. Maintaining a sense of humor is crucial not just for its intrinsic value but also as a tool for empathy. Parents must strive to put themselves in their teenagers' shoes, recalling their own adolescent challenges. This empathetic perspective can pave the way for more open and honest communication.

Finding Joy in Parenting: A Vital Element Often Forgotten

Parents need to enjoy being with their children. This is not just a psychological necessity but also a Scriptural principle. Psalm 127:3 reminds us that "Children are a heritage from Jehovah, the fruit of the womb a reward." If children are a "reward," then the joy of parenting should be self-evident. When parents find joy in spending time with their children, they not only enrich their own lives but also emotionally and spiritually nourish their adolescents.

Averting Pitfalls through Scriptural Wisdom

In conclusion, the Bible provides the framework for successful parenting, even through the potentially treacherous years of adolescence. By avoiding emotional distancing, prioritizing quality family time, maintaining a sense of humor, and discovering joy in the parenting journey, parents can help ensure a spiritually enriching environment for their teenagers. This is pivotal in safeguarding the emotional and spiritual well-being of the family unit.

CHAPTER 11 What You Should Communicate

The Crucial Pillars of Character Development: Honesty, Hard Work, and Proper Conduct

The teenage years represent a watershed moment in the life of an individual. This period is not only marked by physical and emotional changes but also by formative experiences that help shape one's character and worldview. As such, parents have a crucial role to play in ensuring their adolescents develop into mature, ethical adults. According to Scripture, three core values must be impressed upon children: honesty, hard work, and proper conduct. How best can parents instill these values? The Bible offers invaluable guidance in this endeavor.

The Indispensability of Honesty: A Teaching Grounded in 1 Thessalonians 4:11

"If parents have not already inculcated in their children an appreciation for honesty... they should by all means do so during the teen years."

The Apostle Paul exhorts, "Make it your aim to live quietly and to mind your own business and to work with your hands, just as we commanded you" (1 Thessalonians 4:11, UASV). While this verse highlights several virtues, its emphasis on honest living is particularly pertinent for adolescents. *Honesty is not merely an ideal; it is a way of life that has practical implications.* Parents should exemplify honest behavior in all their interactions, thereby showing their teenagers that this virtue is not just theoretical but profoundly consequential in daily life.

The Virtue of Hard Work: Echoes from 2 Thessalonians 3:10

Paul is unequivocal about the necessity of hard work: "For even when we were with you, we used to give you this order: if anyone is not willing to work, then he is not to eat, either" (2 Thessalonians 3:10, UASV). Hard work is not an optional extra but an essential character trait. *Parents need to communicate the value of hard work not merely as a path to material success but also as a means of spiritual and moral edification.* Again, this principle is best communicated through consistent example.

Upholding Moral and Proper Conduct: Wisdom from Proverbs 20:11

It is vital for parents to ensure that their children wholeheartedly believe in the importance of living a moral and clean life. Proverbs 20:11 states, "Even a child makes himself known by his deeds, whether his conduct is pure and upright." Clearly, the Bible underscores the necessity of proper conduct. Parents need to make explicit what is often implicit in daily life by openly discussing what constitutes moral behavior and why it is indispensable.

The Power of Example and Dialogue: Insights from 1 Peter 3:1 and Proverbs 20:5

Example alone is insufficient since children are also exposed to numerous negative influences and seductive messages outside the home. First Peter 3:1 emphasizes the transformative power of conduct, particularly how wives can influence their unbelieving husbands "without a word through the conduct of their wives." This principle is transferable to the parent-teen relationship. However, Proverbs 20:5 stresses the importance of dialogue: "A plan in the heart of a man is like deep water, but a man of understanding draws it out." *Parents must therefore engage in meaningful conversations with their teenagers to understand their views on what they encounter externally.*

The Synergistic Approach

Parents must adopt a synergistic approach that combines example and dialogue in the inculcation of these vital virtues. Honesty, hard work, and proper conduct are not just abstract principles; they are lived realities that adolescents must internalize as they navigate their path to adulthood. By following the biblical prescriptions and combining conduct with meaningful conversation, parents can create a nurturing environment in which their teenagers can grow into morally upright and spiritually mature adults.

The Imperative of Sexual Education: A Biblical Mandate for Parents

In the complex landscape of adolescence, parents face many challenges. Among the most urgent is the imperative to guide their children in understanding sexual matters. This subject, often fraught with discomfort and social taboos, is too significant to be left to external sources that may impart distorted or harmful information. Scripture itself, ever the guiding light in matters of moral and ethical conduct, does not evade discussions of sexuality but approaches them with a spirit of honest instruction. Let's delve into why and how parents should navigate this sensitive but crucial topic.

The Biblical Precedent for Open Dialogue: Insights from Proverbs 4:1-4; 5:1-21

Jehovah is not reticent when it comes to discussing sexual matters in His Word. As Proverbs 5:1-21 demonstrates, He provides specific and unambiguous counsel on avoiding sexual immorality. Verses such as "For the lips of a forbidden woman drip honey, and her speech is smoother than oil" (Proverbs 5:3, UASV) serve as stark warnings about the pitfalls associated with sexual misconduct. Proverbs 4:1-4, in which a father imparts wisdom to his son, further exemplifies the Bible's openness about moral instruction between generations. *If Jehovah Himself does not shy away from such matters, neither should parents.*

The Danger of Leaving Sexual Education to Outsiders

The consequences of failing to educate one's children about sexual matters can be severe. If parents abdicate this responsibility, they run the risk of their children receiving skewed, incomplete, or erroneous information from less reliable sources. *It's not a question of whether children will learn about these matters but from whom and with what level of accuracy and moral integrity.*

Leveraging Existing Resources: The Role of Christian Publishing House Blog and CATEGORY: YOUTHS – 12-25[2]

Christian parents today have a treasure trove of resources available to them that can make the task less daunting. The Christian Publishing House Blog, for instance, has published a wealth of information that aligns with biblical guidance. *Parents should make use of such material to augment their discussions and clarify any misunderstandings.* Reviewing articles in the CATEGORY: YOUTHS – 12-25 with your children can provide structured, faith-based dialogue on the topic. You may indeed be "pleasantly surprised at the results."

Practical Steps for Effective Communication on Sexual Matters

1. **Initiate the Conversation**: Take the first step. Do not wait for your children to come to you; they may never do so.

2. **Be Candid but Appropriate**: Use language and examples that are clear but also age-appropriate. Strive for a balance between honesty and propriety.

3. **Utilize Scripture**: Ground the conversation in what the Bible teaches about sexuality. This will not only lend authority to

---

[2] https://christianpublishinghouse.co/category/youths-12-25/

your words but also emphasize the spiritual significance of sexual conduct.

4. **Employ External Resources Judiciously**: As mentioned, resources like articles from Christian Publishing House Blog can be very useful. However, always ensure that such materials align with Scriptural teachings.

5. **Create a Safe Space for Questions**: Allow your children to ask questions without fear of judgement. This will enable them to clarify any uncertainties and debunk any myths they may have encountered elsewhere.

The Moral Imperative

In summary, the task of educating one's children about sexual matters is a moral imperative that Christian parents cannot afford to ignore. With the support of Scriptural teachings and reliable external resources, parents can navigate this challenging terrain successfully, thereby equipping their children with the understanding and moral fortitude to face the complexities of sexual conduct in today's world.

Cultivating the Service of God in the Hearts of Children: A Comprehensive Approach

There are various subjects that parents and children may discuss, ranging from school to relationships to future plans. However, as Christians, the most important subject that must take precedence in these conversations is the "discipline and instruction of the Lord" (Ephesians 6:4, UASV). This phrase not only encapsulates moral and ethical training but primarily focuses on teaching children how to love and serve God. So, what is the most effective way to accomplish this monumental task? Let's explore this crucial question.

The Apostle Paul's Counsel: A Blueprint for Spiritual Nurturing

The apostle Paul emphasizes the necessity of raising children "in the discipline and instruction of the Lord" (Ephesians 6:4). This is not merely a casual or optional responsibility; it is a Scriptural mandate for Christian parents. The discipline mentioned here pertains to correction and guidance, whereas the instruction is about imparting knowledge and wisdom. Therefore, the most critical subject of discussion between parents and children should be how to serve God effectively.

Teaching by Example: The Primacy of Role Modeling

One of the most potent teaching methods at your disposal is *your own example*. Matthew 22:37 declares that the greatest commandment is to "love your God with your whole heart and with your whole soul and with your whole mind." If your children see that you practice what you preach, that you genuinely love God and express that love through service, worship, and moral conduct, they are far more likely to emulate you. *Children often don't just do as they are told; they do as they see.*

Materialism Versus Spiritual Priorities: Guiding Views on Material Possessions

We live in a world increasingly consumed by material pursuits. In such an environment, the wise words of Ecclesiastes 7:12 stand out: "For wisdom is a protection just as money is a protection, but the advantage of knowledge is that wisdom preserves the life of its owner." Money can buy a measure of security, but it cannot purchase the peace and purpose that come from serving God.

Similarly, Jesus Christ's own words in Matthew 6:31-33 highlight the need to put spiritual pursuits above material ones: "So never be anxious and say, 'What are we to eat?' or, 'What are we to drink?' or, 'What are we to wear?' For all these are the things the nations are eagerly pursuing. Your heavenly Father knows that you need all these things. Keep on, then, seeking first the Kingdom and his righteousness, and all these other things will be added to you."

If your children observe that you prioritize spiritual matters over material pursuits, they are more likely to internalize these values.

Practical Steps for Effective Teaching on Serving God

1. **Consistent Family Worship**: Regularly study the Bible together. Make this a non-negotiable family time where you discuss Scripture and how to apply it in your lives.

2. **Involvement in Church Activities**: Engage in church services, bible studies, and other spiritual activities as a family.

3. **Service Opportunities**: Look for ways to serve others as a family. Acts of kindness and community service are practical ways to express your love for God and cultivate the same in your children.

4. **Open and Honest Communication**: Always have an open line of communication about their doubts, questions, and thoughts regarding their faith. *Your willingness to discuss and explore will make them feel secure in coming to you with their spiritual concerns.*

5. **Prayer**: Pray as a family and encourage individual prayers. This will help your children to develop a personal relationship with God.

A Life-Long Commitment

Teaching your children to serve God is a lifelong commitment. It is not something that can be done haphazardly or left to chance. It requires intentionality, consistency, and above all, the exemplary power of your own life in service to God. By prioritizing spiritual values over material concerns, and by openly expressing your love for God in both word and deed, you set a powerful example for your children to follow. This will not only benefit them in this life but, more importantly, will guide their steps on the path to eternal life.

The Essentials for a Successful Family Bible Study

Embarking on a journey of spiritual education within the family requires meticulous planning and a conscientious approach. A family Bible study serves as an instrumental means to imbue spiritual values and Scriptural understanding in young people (Psalm 119:33, 34; Proverbs 4:20-23). In this endeavor, there are specific points that must be kept in mind for the family Bible study to be genuinely impactful.

Prioritization and Regularity: The Cornerstones of Family Bible Study

The psalmist speaks to the value of meditating on God's laws day and night and being like a tree planted by the rivers of water (Psalm 1:1-3). Consistency and regularity are not just good ideas; they're Scriptural imperatives for spiritual growth. The family Bible study must not be treated as an optional or secondary activity but should be considered a priority around which other activities are scheduled. *The regularity of these studies forms the backbone of spiritual development within the household.*

Creating the Right Atmosphere: A Blend of Respect and Relaxation

The atmosphere of the family Bible study plays an instrumental role in its efficacy. It must be balanced—informal to encourage open dialogue, yet respectful to maintain the seriousness of what's being studied. *The atmosphere should neither be so rigid as to stifle conversation nor so lax as to become counterproductive.* Striking this balance can be a challenge, but as one father noted, even when things don't go perfectly, the aim should be to persevere and look toward making the next session better.

Praying for Divine Guidance: Invoking God's Blessing

It's crucial to involve God in your efforts. The same father advised that he begins each study with a prayer specifically asking for God's guidance for everyone involved (Psalm 119:66). This aligns everyone's hearts and minds and invites divine intervention for an effective study. *Prayer serves as a spiritual alignment tool, ensuring that the study is not just an academic exercise but a spiritually enriching experience.*

The Parental Role: Responsibility and Adaptability

Conducting the family study is primarily the responsibility of believing parents. While some parents may not be gifted teachers, their sincere effort to make the study interesting can still be highly effective. Your children, especially teenagers, may not always express enthusiasm, but if you love them "in deed and truth," your deep interest in their spiritual welfare will come across (1 John 3:18).

Strategies for Keeping It Engaging

1. **Interactive Methods**: Use questions, quizzes, or even small enactments to make the study more interactive.
2. **Real-world Applications**: Make sure to relate the lessons to real-world scenarios that your teenagers might encounter, thereby making the Bible relevant to them.
3. **Let Them Lead**: Occasionally, allow the children to lead the study or choose the topic, thereby giving them a sense of ownership.

A Commitment to Spiritual Growth

While conducting a successful family Bible study may come with its set of challenges, the benefits far outweigh the difficulties. Consistency, the right atmosphere, and divine guidance can serve as your North Stars as you navigate this vital spiritual endeavor. Your earnestness and humility in helping your teenagers grow spiritually will not only honor God but will also lay a solid foundation for their faith.

Applying Deuteronomy 11:18, 19 in Communicating Spiritual Things to Teenagers

The spiritual nourishment of our young ones is not confined to any single setting or activity. Deuteronomy 11:18, 19 is a timeless passage that provides an essential framework for imparting spiritual values to our offspring. It doesn't merely suggest that these instructions be reserved for Sabbath days, religious gatherings, or structured family Bible studies. It calls for a more expansive, all-encompassing approach. Let us delve into how these verses can be operationalized in today's context, especially when communicating with teenagers.

Integrate Spiritual Matters into Everyday Life

"You must also teach them to your sons, so as to speak of them when you sit in your house and when you walk on the road and when you lie down and when you get up," says the passage (Deuteronomy 11:19). Here, the Scripture points to four different scenarios: sitting in your house, walking on the road, lying down, and getting up. These refer to a comprehensive lifestyle, one where *spiritual matters are seamlessly integrated into the daily routine.*

Be Opportunistic, Not Overbearing

It's essential to understand that Deuteronomy 11:18, 19 does not advocate a constant preaching or lecture mode, which could be counterproductive, especially with teenagers. Instead, parents should adopt an opportunistic approach. This means *being vigilant and discerning to seize "teachable moments" as they arise naturally* during the course of daily life.

Sign Upon Your Hand, Frontlet Between Your Eyes: A Metaphor for Conscious Action and Focus

When the passage refers to binding these words as "a sign upon your hand" and as "a frontlet band between your eyes," it employs a metaphor. The "hand" is often symbolic of action, and "between your eyes" suggests focus or attention. The metaphor suggests that spiritual matters should not only be something you think about but also something you act upon. Parents need to *exemplify these values in their own lives* to serve as effective role models.

Open Dialogue: Involve Them in Conversations, Don't Preach

Deuteronomy 6:6, 7 echoes similar sentiments about keeping these words on your heart and repeating them to your children. Instead of treating spiritual conversations as a monologue, involve your teenagers in a dialogue. Ask for their opinions, questions, and interpretations of Scripture. Make it an *interactive learning experience*, thus engaging them more deeply.

Use Current Events and Real-life Scenarios as Launching Points

Given that the instruction is to discuss these matters "when you walk on the road," this could imply that even when you're engaged in mundane or routine activities, you can utilize current events or real-life scenarios to provoke spiritual contemplation. It could be a news story that lines up with Biblical principles or a moral dilemma one of their peers is facing.

In Summary: A Lifelong Commitment to Spiritual Enrichment

The command in Deuteronomy isn't just a set of guidelines; it's a lifestyle—a continuous, conscious commitment to spiritual nurturing that goes beyond formal settings. This Scriptural counsel is as relevant today as it was when first given. The goal is to instill spiritual principles so deeply that they become an integral part of the child's character, aiding them as they navigate the challenges of teenage years and beyond.

Edward D. Andrews

CHAPTER 12 Discipline and Respect

Understanding the Nature and Necessity of Discipline in a Christian Home

In the framework of a Christian home, discipline is a critical component that parents are mandated to exercise in the upbringing of their children. Discipline is often misunderstood or misconceived as mere punishment, but it encompasses far more than that. The Bible provides guidance on what discipline is and how it should be conducted in the context of the family.

Defining Discipline: More Than Punishment

At its core, *discipline is training that corrects and molds character*. It includes teaching, reproof, correction, and, yes, sometimes, punishment. However, the primary focus should be on *correction and constructive change rather than mere retribution*. This aligns with the Scriptural understanding as seen in Proverbs 22:6: "Train up a child in the way he should go; even when he is old, he will not depart from it."

Discipline Involves Communication

Effective discipline is a two-way street that involves open and respectful *communication between parents and children*. It's not just dictating do's and don'ts but rather discussing the reasons and the underlying values behind the rules. This fosters not just obedience but understanding, as commanded in Ephesians 6:4: "Go on bringing [your children] up in the discipline and instruction of the Lord."

Discipline Throughout Development: Childhood to Adolescence

Children needed discipline when they were younger, and it's a myth to think that the need dissipates as they grow into teenagers. In fact, they may need it *even more so* during these years when they are grappling with greater challenges and making choices that could affect the rest of their lives. Wise adolescents realize the value of constructive discipline in helping them navigate these complicated years.

Discipline Must be Balanced

Too little discipline could lead to permissiveness, a lack of respect, and poor choices on the part of the child. On the other hand, excessive punishment without constructive teaching can result in resentment and rebellion. *Balance is key*, as suggested by the apostle Paul in Colossians 3:21: "Fathers, do not provoke your children, lest they become discouraged."

The Ultimate Aim: A Godly Character

The ultimate aim of discipline should be to instill a godly character in our children, to enable them to stand "complete and fully assured in all the will of God" (Colossians 4:12). That's why discipline should be consistent, fair, rooted in love, and aimed at moral and spiritual development.

Discipline is a comprehensive strategy involving training, communication, and sometimes punishment aimed at molding godly character. Its necessity spans the development stages from childhood to adolescence. When executed with wisdom, balance, and love, discipline serves as an irreplaceable tool in fulfilling our God-given role as parents. It lays the foundation for our children not merely to become functional adults but to become lifelong servants of God.

The Biblical Framework for Administering and Heeding Discipline

Scripture provides a detailed blueprint regarding who should administer discipline and who has the onus to heed it. In the Christian household, discipline is not just an optional practice but a divine mandate for character development and spiritual growth.

Responsibility for Administering Discipline: Primarily the Parents, Especially the Father

In the biblical framework, *the primary responsibility for administering discipline falls on the parents*, with a particular emphasis on the role of the father. This aligns with Ephesians 6:4, which states, "Go on bringing [your children] up in the discipline and instruction of the Lord." The term "father" here is not just a designation of a biological relationship but denotes the role of spiritual headship and moral authority in the home. Fathers are instructed not to provoke their children to anger but to raise them with the training and instruction appropriate to a reverent life (Ephesians 6:4; Colossians 3:21).

But while the father carries significant weight in this area, the mother also plays an essential role. The Bible exhorts children to heed the teaching of both their father and their mother. Proverbs 1:8 amplifies this: "Listen, my son, to your father's instruction, and do not forsake the teaching of your mother." Therefore, *both parents should be engaged* in the discipline and moral education of their children.

Responsibility to Heed Discipline: Rests with the Teenager

The *responsibility for listening to and heeding that discipline squarely rests on the shoulders of the teenager.* Proverbs 15:5 makes this clear: "Anyone foolish disrespects the discipline of his father, but anyone regarding reproof is shrewd." This verse not only encourages teenagers to heed discipline but also implies that such discipline will indeed be administered.

Furthering this, Proverbs 13:18 asserts, "The one neglecting discipline comes to poverty and dishonor, but the one keeping a reproof is the one that is glorified." This Scripture emphasizes the high stakes involved in either disregarding or adhering to discipline. *Failure to heed discipline can lead to adverse outcomes, both morally and practically*, while respecting reproof can result in a life that is "glorified," or well-regarded and fulfilling.

Mutual Accountability

While the parents, particularly the father, have the role of administering discipline, and the teenager has the responsibility to heed it, *there is a sense of mutual accountability*. Parents are accountable to God for how they administer discipline, and teenagers are accountable for how they respond to it. Therefore, this is not merely a human interaction but one that has spiritual implications and accountability before God.

The Bible is unambiguous: God entrusts the responsibility for administering discipline to parents, particularly fathers. Meanwhile, the onus for heeding this discipline lies with the teenagers. Both parties have a divinely ordained role, and the successful execution of these roles is crucial for the spiritual and moral development of the family. When parents administer wise and loving discipline, and when teenagers heed it, the entire family grows in wisdom and stature, and in favor with God and people (Luke 2:52).

The Delicate Balance in Administering Discipline: Neither Too Strict Nor Too Permissive

Disciplining teenagers is a complex and often challenging task that requires considerable wisdom, discernment, and emotional intelligence. Achieving a balanced approach is crucial. The Bible offers invaluable guidance in this area, offering principles that parents can apply in their efforts to discipline their children effectively, yet lovingly.

The Danger of Excessive Strictness: Irritation and Damaged Self-Confidence

One of the pitfalls parents need to avoid is *being overly strict or authoritarian*, which can lead to irritation and even damage a child's self-confidence. Colossians 3:21 warns against this, stating, "Fathers, do not provoke your children, so they will not become disheartened." The term "provoke" here can include being overly harsh, punitive, or restrictive.

Being excessively strict can have the counterproductive effect of instilling fear rather than respect, and resentment rather than obedience. It may quench a child's spirit and negatively impact their emotional and psychological well-being. Therefore, it is imperative that *strictness does not overshadow grace and love* in the discipline process.

The Pitfall of Excessive Leniency: Missing Out on Vital Training

On the other end of the spectrum lies the danger of *being too lenient or permissive*. A too-permissive approach can deprive the child of the valuable life skills and moral principles that discipline instills. Proverbs 29:17 illustrates the value of appropriate discipline: "Chastise your son and he will bring you rest and give much pleasure to your soul." Discipline serves a constructive purpose; it is designed to correct, train, and ultimately bring "rest" and "pleasure" to the family unit.

However, excessive leniency can be disastrous. Proverbs 29:21 gives a cautionary note: "If one is pampering one's servant from youth on, in his later life he will even become a thankless one." While this verse initially addresses the treatment of a servant, its principle *applies with equal measure to any youngster in the household*. Pampering or excessive leniency can result in a lack of gratitude, a sense of entitlement, and various other negative behavioral traits.

The Balanced Approach: Firm yet Compassionate Discipline

So, what does a balanced approach look like? It is a combination of *firmness and compassion, structure and flexibility, expectations and empathy*. It's about setting clear boundaries while also giving room for freedom within those boundaries. It means administering consequences when necessary but also extending grace and forgiveness.

This balanced approach aligns with the Scriptural principle found in Ephesians 6:4: "Go on bringing [your children] up in the discipline and instruction of the Lord." This includes not only rules and regulations but also mentorship, coaching, and the nurturing of a personal relationship with God.

Achieving a balanced approach to discipline is both an art and a science, requiring wisdom that often comes from a combination of Scriptural insight and practical experience. By avoiding the extremes of both harshness and permissiveness, parents can aim to administer discipline that is *both loving and effective*, fulfilling the divine mandate to bring their children up "in the discipline and instruction of the Lord."

Discipline as a Manifestation of Love and Its Impact on Household Stability

Discipline is not merely an action; it is an expression. It is a tangible way in which parents manifest their love and concern for their children's well-being, both immediate and future. This concept is deeply rooted in biblical principles, and its application has far-reaching implications for the family unit.

Discipline as a Proof of Parental Love

Scripture makes it clear that *discipline is an evidence of love*. Hebrews 12:6 states, "For those whom the Lord loves he disciplines, and scourges every son whom he receives." Later in the same chapter, verse 11 explains, "No discipline seems enjoyable at the time, but painful. Later on, however, it yields the peaceful fruit of righteousness to those who have been trained by it."

It is essential to understand that discipline isn't about exerting control but about *guiding the child towards righteousness and responsible behavior*. In other words, discipline is not so much about penalizing bad behavior as it is about fostering good behavior. It aims at the holistic development of the child, aligning with God's standards and leading to "the peaceful fruit of righteousness."

The Peril of Inconsistent Discipline: An Unstable Household

On the flip side, a lack of consistent discipline can lead to severe consequences for the family unit. Proverbs 29:15 provides a warning in this regard: "A rod and a reprimand impart wisdom, but a child left undisciplined disgraces his mother." When discipline is neglected, the household risks falling into chaos. The phrase *"a child left undisciplined"* implies not just the absence of discipline but a lack of consistent, reasoned discipline. This can result in a household "that is out of control," as the children lack the boundaries and guidelines that help them navigate life responsibly.

Additionally, Galatians 6:9 underscores the importance of not becoming weary in doing good, which includes the taxing but rewarding work of consistently disciplining children. It states, "Let us not grow weary of doing good, for in due season we will reap, if we do not give up." For parents, it might sometimes seem easier, at least in the short term, to allow an obstinate teenager to have his or her way. However, this convenience comes at a cost: the long-term stability and spiritual health of the household.

Consistency Is Key to Effective, Loving Discipline

Discipline, therefore, serves dual purposes. It is both an act of love from the parent and an essential framework for the child. A parent's willingness to administer consistent discipline, even when it is challenging to do so, is a testament to their genuine love and concern for their child's well-being. Furthermore, this consistent discipline ensures that the household remains a stable environment, one that honors God and nurtures the souls who reside within it. Therefore, *for the sake of both love and peace, parents are encouraged to be steadfast in their disciplinary actions*, undergirded by biblical principles.

CHAPTER 13 Work and Recreation for Teenagers

The Wisdom of Navigating Teenagers' Recreational Choices

As parents, one of the significant challenges faced is how to guide teenagers in their recreational activities. In our contemporary society, unsupervised leisure time has significantly increased compared to previous generations, who were usually expected to contribute more directly to household chores or agricultural tasks. Coupled with the secular world's allure through an array of leisurely activities that often disregard Scriptural moral standards, this presents a potential pitfall for our youth.

The Role of Parents in Supervising Recreational Choices

According to the biblical model, *parents bear the ultimate responsibility* for ensuring that their children's activities align with Christian principles. Ephesians 6:4 provides an essential guideline, stating, "Fathers, do not provoke your children to anger, but bring them up in the discipline and instruction of the Lord." This verse emphasizes that parents are not merely supervisors but also educators in their children's lives.

The judicious parent maintains the right to make final decisions about recreation. While it is tempting to leave children to their devices, especially as they age and desire more independence, the parental role should not diminish but adapt. The challenge lies in balancing control with allowing increasing latitude as your child matures.

Gradual Increase of Autonomy Reflecting Spiritual Maturity

As teenagers grow, they naturally seek more independence and autonomy, including in their choices of recreation. *It's crucial to recognize and respect this developmental stage while guiding them towards righteous choices.* The ultimate goal is to see the child make decisions that reflect "progress toward spiritual maturity." This idea aligns with the Apostle Paul's teaching in 1 Corinthians 13:11: "When I was a child, I spoke like a child, I thought like a child, I reasoned like a child. When I became a man, I gave up childish ways."

Therefore, *allowing more latitude in recreation should be directly proportional to their spiritual maturity.* This doesn't mean they will always make the right decisions, especially in areas that are filled with worldly temptations, such as the kind of music they listen to or the friends they choose to associate with.

Addressing Unwise Choices Through Open Dialogue

When unwise choices inevitably occur, these should become opportunities for teaching rather than mere occasions for punishment. In the spirit of Proverbs 22:6—"Train up a child in the way he should go; even when he is old he will not depart from it"—*these moments should be discussed openly with the teenager.* The goal is to help them understand why their choices were unwise and guide them towards making better decisions in the future, rather than alienating them with harsh reprimands.

The Delicate Balance of Control and Freedom

Navigating the labyrinth of teenagers' recreational choices is a task requiring wisdom, tact, and a thorough grounding in Scriptural principles. As parents, you have the God-given responsibility to guide your children in a world increasingly at odds with Christian morality. By maintaining a firm yet loving hand on the reins, especially in these formative years, you are setting the stage not just for a peaceful household, but for spiritually mature adults who honor God with their lives.

The Principle of Reasonableness in Time Allocation for Recreation

In an era where many are led to believe that life should be a constant stream of entertainment and pleasure, the concept of *reasonableness* in recreation becomes pivotal, especially for teenagers. The Bible warns about the dangers of indulging too much in the "pleasures of this life," which have the potential to choke out the importance and impact of God's Word (Luke 8:11-15). Thus, a balance needs to be struck, and parents have a crucial role to play in this.

The Pitfall of Excessive Recreation

In many modern societies, the norm is leaning towards an excessive focus on recreational activities, which poses significant risks. When a teenager's life revolves solely around seeking one form of entertainment after another, they risk neglecting other crucial aspects of life and growth. *Being engrossed in constant recreation can create an imbalance that hampers spiritual, emotional, and intellectual development.*

The Parental Role in Teaching Reasonableness

Parents have the responsibility to inculcate in their children a sense of balance and priority, grounded in biblical principles. Ephesians 5:15-16 advises, "Look carefully then how you walk, not as unwise but as wise, making the best use of the time because the days are evil." Parents should help teenagers understand that time is a valuable resource given by God, and it needs to be used wisely.

Teaching reasonableness involves showing teenagers that their schedule should include a variety of activities necessary for balanced growth. *Time should be allocated for family interaction, personal Bible study, association with spiritually mature individuals, participation in Christian meetings, and even household chores.* These activities contribute to a well-rounded personality and help instill values and skills that are important for life.

The Protective Factor of Reasonableness

Being reasonable in the amount of time spent in recreation serves as a protective barrier. It guards against several dangers:

1. **Spiritual Danger**: Constant recreation can lead to spiritual stagnation or regression. By limiting such activities, the teenager remains alert to spiritual needs and is more likely to grow in faith.
2. **Emotional and Social Risks**: A life focused solely on pleasure often lacks depth. Emotional and social skills are developed through interactions in a variety of settings, including the home and church.
3. **Intellectual Growth**: Time spent on personal study, chores, and other constructive activities contributes to intellectual development, giving the individual a broader perspective on life.
4. **Physical Health**: Excessive recreation, especially of the sedentary kind, can also have negative health implications. A balanced life usually leads to better physical health.

The Wisdom of Balance

Being reasonable with the time spent in recreation is not about robbing a teenager of fun experiences, but about enriching their lives with a range of activities that contribute to holistic development. By teaching them to prioritize time wisely, parents prepare their teenagers for a fulfilling, responsible, and spiritually rewarding adult life.

The Importance of Balancing Recreation with Other Aspects of Life

King Solomon, endowed with wisdom from Jehovah, provides invaluable insight into the subject of life balance in Ecclesiastes 3:12-13. These verses affirm that *rejoicing is a good thing*, but they also emphasize the importance of *hard work*. Understanding and maintaining this balance is essential, not just for adults but also for teenagers who are navigating a critical phase of their lives.

The Necessity of Hard Work

In an age where instant gratification often takes center stage, many teenagers have not experienced the deep satisfaction that comes from sustained, hard work. Whether it is solving a challenging problem, mastering a new skill, or dedicating time and energy to a worthwhile cause, hard work brings with it a *sense of accomplishment and self-respect* that is both unique and fulfilling. The Bible makes it clear that hard work is not just a duty but a gift from God (Ecclesiastes 3:13).

Developing Skills and Trades

One challenge parents face is ensuring that their teenagers are exposed to opportunities where they can develop a skill or trade that will be useful in their future lives. Proverbs 22:6 emphasizes this: "Train up a child in the way he should go; even when he is old he will not depart from it." Teaching a teenager the *value of hard work and the joy of mastery* is a critical life skill that equips them for adulthood. This is especially important in a world where many lack the basic skills to support themselves.

Other Important Balancing Factors

1. **Spiritual Growth**: The Apostle Paul noted that physical training has some value, but spiritual training is valuable for this life and the life to come (1 Timothy 4:8). A balanced life

should involve personal Bible study, prayer, and participation in Christian meetings and activities.

2. **Educational Commitments**: The Bible highlights the value of wisdom and understanding (Proverbs 4:7). Hence, academic commitments should not be overlooked.

3. **Family Time**: Good family relationships are important for mental and emotional health. Time spent with family also allows parents to impart valuable life skills and moral teachings to their children (Deuteronomy 6:6-9).

4. **Community and Charity**: In line with Galatians 6:10, it's also vital to balance recreation with opportunities to "do good to all people." This can instill a sense of empathy and social responsibility in the teenager.

The Parental Challenge: Instilling a Healthy Outlook

Parents have a monumental but rewarding task at hand. The objective is not merely to restrict or permit certain activities but to imbue their teenagers with a *holistic understanding of what a balanced life entails*. If parents can succeed in teaching their teenager to value hard work and the other balancing factors mentioned above, they will have equipped them with a healthy life outlook that will bring long-lasting benefits.

CHAPTER 14 From Teenager to Adult

The Transition from Teenager to Adult: The Indispensable Role of Encouragement

The transition from adolescence to adulthood is fraught with challenges and opportunities. It is a time when parental guidance is still needed, yet the urge for independence is at an all-time high. This tension can create both conflict and opportunity for growth within the family. *The cornerstone of navigating this complex landscape is undeniably love*, a truth rooted deeply in the wisdom of 1 Corinthians 13:8, which tells us that "Love never fails."

Consistent and Affirming Love

In the relational dynamics between parents and teenagers, love should be the constant that never wavers, regardless of the circumstances. This is not merely a passive form of love but an active, *intentional commitment to the well-being of the teenager*. Love manifests itself in various ways — one of which is consistent encouragement.

Seizing Opportunities for Positive Reinforcement

Parents should be vigilant in recognizing and praising their child's successes, no matter how small. These could range from overcoming a personal hurdle to achieving something noteworthy. The power of positive reinforcement is supported by Philippians 4:8, which encourages us to think about whatever is true, honorable, and commendable. By *highlighting the positive*, parents reinforce the kind of behavior and attitude that will serve their children well in adulthood.

Expressing Love and Appreciation

As parents, it's easy to get caught up in the whirlwind of daily responsibilities and challenges. But opportunities to express love and appreciation for your teenager should never be passed up. The emotional and psychological well-being of a teenager is significantly enhanced when they feel valued and loved. The Bible is filled with examples of affectionate, encouraging relationships, such as that between Jonathan and David (1 Samuel 18:1-3), characterized by mutual love and respect.

The Return of Love

Children, including teenagers, tend to mirror the love they receive. The principle found in Luke 6:31, often referred to as the Golden Rule, is applicable here: "As you wish that others would do to you, do so to them." When teenagers are secure in the love they receive, they are not only more likely to return that love but also to act in ways that make them worthy of love.

Navigating Misunderstandings

Misunderstandings and conflicts are inevitable. However, they can be mitigated and often resolved when both parties know that the underlying love is unconditional. The love parents have for their children should emulate the agape love described in the Scriptures — selfless, unconditional, and enduring.

The Parental Objective: A Loving, Enduring Relationship

The goal is not merely to navigate the teenage years with minimal conflict but to set the stage for a *long-term, loving relationship that persists into adulthood.* This requires a multifaceted approach rooted in love, active encouragement, and seizing every opportunity to uplift and affirm the teenager. The enduring wisdom of Scripture serves as an infallible guide in this most crucial endeavor.

So, parents, regularly ask yourselves: 'Do I compliment each child on his successes in handling problems or overcoming obstacles? Do I seize opportunities to express my love and appreciation for my children before those opportunities pass?' A positive answer to these questions will make the often-challenging teenage years not merely bearable but fruitful, enriching the family unit as a whole.

The Balance of Free Will and Parental Guidance: A Scriptural Examination

The task of raising children to be righteous adults is monumental and fraught with challenges. The Bible provides an invaluable roadmap for parents on this journey. A cornerstone principle in this regard is found in Proverbs 22:6: "*Train up a boy according to the way for him; even when he grows old he will not turn aside from it.*"

Proverbs 22:6: A General Rule, Not An Absolute Guarantee

This passage is often cited as a go-to formula for successful parenting. However, it's critical to understand that while Proverbs 22:6 provides a foundational guideline, it is not an absolute guarantee. This Proverb offers a *general principle*, not a *universal promise*. This distinction is crucial for parents to bear in mind, especially when faced with the complexities of human free will.

The Unpredictability of Free Will

Scripture acknowledges that humans, like angelic beings, have the gift of free will. This means children can make choices that are contrary to their upbringing, as evidenced in the rebellion of some of Jehovah's spirit sons (Genesis 6:2; Jude 6). It's a sobering reminder that *children are not programmable entities but beings with their own free will, accountable to Jehovah.*

Personal Responsibility Before God

Each individual, as they grow into adulthood, becomes personally accountable for their actions before God. This is an inviolable principle that aligns with the objective Historical-Grammatical method of biblical interpretation. Parents may guide, train, and nurture, but at the end of the day, each person makes their own choices and must face the consequences of those choices.

Navigating The Complexities of Parental Aspirations and Child Choices

As a parent, you might witness your child make decisions that are deeply troubling, such as turning away from serving God. In such cases, remember that even Jehovah experienced rebellion from His own spirit sons. Your faithfulness and your relationship with Jehovah are not invalidated by the choices your child makes. Your role is to do your best to "train up" your child, instilling the principles and values that honor Jehovah.

So, what should be borne in mind? Proverbs 22:6 stands as a guiding principle that generally holds true: good training usually leads to a good outcome. Yet, the existence of free will means there are no guarantees. Each child will ultimately stand responsible for their own decisions before God. A wise parent holds these two truths in tension, continuing to love, guide, and pray for their children, no matter the choices they make. This dual acknowledgment of scriptural principle and the reality of free will allows parents to approach the challenges of raising children with both hope and realism.

Gratitude to God Through Godly Parenthood: An In-Depth Scriptural Examination

Parenthood is a profound responsibility and a divine privilege. It's not just about bringing life into the world; it's about nurturing that life in the "discipline and instruction of the Lord" (Ephesians 6:4, UASV). How parents approach this sacred duty is indeed a testament to their gratitude toward God for entrusting them with such an invaluable gift.

Demonstrating Love: The Core of Godly Parenting

The Apostle Paul reminds us that "*Love never fails*" (1 Corinthians 13:8, UASV). This truth must be at the heart of Christian parenting. A child's perception of God is often formed through their relationship with their parents. By showing consistent, unconditional love, parents can exemplify the steadfast love of God, creating a household environment where the principles of Scripture can flourish.

Adherence to Bible Principles: The Framework for Parental Guidance

It is not enough to claim a love for God; it must be demonstrated through action. The Apostle John clarifies this when he says, "*This is the love of God, that we keep His commandments*" (1 John 5:3, UASV). Teaching your children to adhere to biblical principles in every facet of life—from honesty to kindness to obedience to God's standards—is essential. These principles act as a moral compass, guiding your children in a world often adrift from spiritual truth.

Setting a Godly Example: Living the Principles You Teach

Children are perceptive and tend to mimic the behavior of their elders. It's not just what you say but what you do that leaves an indelible mark on their character. Paul, who wrote a good number of

New Testament epistles, including the letter to the Hebrews, underscores the importance of setting a good example when he says, "*Be imitators of me, just as I also am of Christ*" (1 Corinthians 11:1, UASV). The most effective teaching is often done without words, through living a life of integrity and godliness.

The Pinnacle of Grateful Stewardship

In the final analysis, the finest way for parents to show gratitude to God for the gift of parenthood is to commit to being godly parents. This involves a threefold strategy: demonstrating love, adhering to biblical principles, and setting a godly example. This not only aligns with the objective Historical-Grammatical method of interpreting the Bible but also gives children the best chance to grow into responsible, God-fearing adults. In doing so, you are effectively returning the gift of life back to God, shaped and nurtured in His ways. This is the ultimate form of gratitude any parent can offer to God for the inestimable privilege of parenthood.

The Imperative of Understanding: Guiding Principles for Parenting Teenagers

In navigating the complex landscape of parenting, especially in the tumultuous teenage years, the Bible offers an indispensable source of wisdom. The quintessential cornerstone for a healthy parent-teen relationship is understanding, which can only be achieved through effective communication.

The Value of Communication: Wisdom from Proverbs

The Bible provides sound advice in Proverbs 15:22: "*Without consultation, plans are frustrated, but with many counselors, they succeed.*" (UASV) This principle can be extended to the familial context, emphasizing the need for parents and teenagers to engage in open, honest dialogue. While it's true that the parent holds authority in the home, understanding is a two-way street. Seeking counsel and discussion with your teenager can yield plans and decisions that are beneficial to both parties.

Note the Importance of Two-Way Communication

When we say communication is needed, we are not advocating a one-way dictation of rules and standards. Far from it! *Parents should be listeners as much as they are speakers.* Teenagers are at a stage where they are grappling with identity, peer pressure, and moral choices. Listening to them not only fosters respect but also provides a nuanced understanding that can be invaluable in guiding them appropriately.

Understanding Emotional and Psychological Changes

The Bible acknowledges the complexities of the human condition. For instance, King Solomon reflects on the various seasons of human life in Ecclesiastes 3. The teenage years are a "season" filled with rapid emotional and psychological changes. *Understanding these changes is critical in providing the emotional support that teenagers so desperately need.*

Balancing Discipline and Freedom

Paul instructs in Ephesians 6:4: "*Fathers, do not provoke your children to anger, but bring them up in the discipline and instruction of the Lord.*" (UASV) The emphasis here is on a balanced approach to child-rearing. While discipline and instruction are essential, they must not be to the extent of provoking your children. *Parents need to understand that too much restriction can be counterproductive.* An atmosphere of understanding fosters trust, a cornerstone for a balanced approach to discipline and freedom.

Spiritual Guidance and Values

Finally, parents must not neglect the spiritual formation of their teenagers. Timothy's mother and grandmother are cited as godly influences in his young life (2 Timothy 1:5). They likely understood his spiritual needs and guided him appropriately. In the same vein, *parents must seek to understand their teenager's spiritual questions, doubts, and needs* to provide relevant guidance.

The Covenant of Understanding

In conclusion, *the core tenet of effective parenting, particularly during the teenage years, is understanding*, facilitated by open communication, emotional support, balanced discipline, and spiritual guidance. All these can be gleaned from the rich well of wisdom that is the Bible. By following these principles, parents are well-positioned to guide their teenagers through one of the most challenging periods of growth and self-discovery, bringing to life the wisdom encapsulated in Proverbs 15:22.

The Individuality Principle: Recognizing Each Teen as Unique

As children transition into the teenage years, they begin a quest to discover their unique identities. During this crucial period, the role of parents is more significant than ever. One of the most fundamental needs that teenagers have is to be recognized and treated as individuals. The Bible provides time-honored wisdom for this aspect of parenting as well.

Biblical Understanding of Individual Worth

Scripture is replete with examples and principles that emphasize the individual worth of a person. In Psalm 139:13-14, David declares, "*For you formed my inward parts; you knitted me together in my mother's womb. I praise you, for I am fearfully and wonderfully made.*" (UASV) This passage serves as a vivid reminder that each child is a unique creation of God, deserving to be treated as such.

Recognize Individual Talents and Interests

It is crucial for parents to recognize and nurture the unique talents, gifts, and interests that God has placed in each child. Romans 12:6-8 speaks about the diversity of gifts among believers. While this is in the context of the church body, the principle extends to the family unit. *Parents should help their teenagers discover their God-given talents and interests, and provide opportunities for them to cultivate these gifts.*

The Pitfall of Comparisons

The Bible warns against the dangers of making comparisons. Paul in 2 Corinthians 10:12 warns, "*When they measure themselves by themselves and compare themselves with themselves, they are without understanding.*" This is a principle that parents should bear in mind. *Comparing your teenager to siblings or to other teenagers can be both emotionally and psychologically damaging.*

The Prodigal Son: A Lesson in Individual Treatment

The parable of the Prodigal Son in Luke 15:11-32 provides valuable insights. In this story, the father deals with each of his sons according to their individual needs and character. The younger son needed forgiveness and restoration, while the older son needed a lesson in grace and humility. The father did not employ a one-size-fits-all approach; instead, he addressed each son's individual needs. *Parents can learn from this by not employing a one-size-fits-all parenting approach but adapting their parenting strategies according to the individual character and needs of each teenager.*

Empathy and Open Communication

Effective communication is crucial in treating your teenager as an individual. James 1:19 advises, "*You must understand this, my beloved: let every person be quick to hear, slow to speak, slow to anger.*" Parents should be willing to listen to their teenager's individual concerns, fears, and aspirations. *Understanding can only be achieved when there is open communication.*

Conclusion: The Importance of Individuality in Parenting

In sum, the Bible provides a rich tapestry of principles and examples that underline the importance of recognizing the individuality of each teenager. This involves acknowledging their unique gifts, avoiding harmful comparisons, adapting parenting strategies to each child's unique needs, and fostering an environment of open communication. These steps, grounded in Scriptural principles, can significantly impact the emotional and spiritual development of teenagers.

The Principle of Consistency: Establishing Stable Guidelines for Teenagers

In a world filled with chaos, inconsistency, and moral relativity, what teenagers often crave, whether they articulate it or not, is consistency—especially from their parents. The Bible provides a wealth of instruction and principles that parents can apply in setting consistent guidelines for their teenagers.

The Bible on Consistency

One of the most seminal verses that underscore the importance of consistency in training children is Proverbs 22:6: "*Train up a boy according to the way for him; even when he grows old he will not turn aside from it.*" (UASV) This verse lays the groundwork for the need to establish stable, consistent guidelines and principles that can steer teenagers through the turbulent waters of adolescence into the safe harbors of adulthood.

The Importance of Consistency

Consistency breeds a sense of security and stability. Teenagers are in a stage of life characterized by many changes: physical, emotional, and spiritual. In such a phase, the consistent guidelines set by parents act as an anchor. *Inconsistent rules and guidelines can lead to confusion, insecurity, and a lack of trust.*

Consequences Must Also Be Consistent

In his letter to the Ephesians, the Apostle Paul writes, "*Fathers, do not provoke your children to anger, but bring them up in the discipline and instruction of the Lord*" (Ephesians 6:4). This underscores the necessity for consistency not only in guidelines but also in consequences. *Discipline that is fair, balanced, and consistent is far more effective than discipline that is erratic or capricious.*

Modeling Consistency: Living What You Preach

It's important to remember that guidelines aren't just about rules; they're also about modeling consistent Christian behavior. In 1 Corinthians 11:1, Paul says, "*Be imitators of me, just as I also am of Christ.*" This principle suggests that parents need to model the behavior they expect. *Guidelines and expectations lose their weight if parents themselves do not abide by them.*

Maintaining Flexibility within Consistency

While consistency is vital, so is the ability to adapt guidelines to meet individual needs and situations. James 3:17 speaks of the wisdom from above being "willing to yield," suggesting a balance between being consistent and making necessary adjustments for individual circumstances. *Consistency should not be confused with rigidity.*

The Biblical Mandate for Consistent Parenting

The Bible provides a strong foundation for the principle of consistency in parenting. Through steady guidelines and consistent consequences, parents can create an environment that fosters emotional and spiritual growth in their teenagers. However, it is equally important for parents to live consistently with the values and principles they wish to instill in their children. In doing so, they build not only obedient but also God-fearing adults, fully equipped for every good work (2 Timothy 3:16-17).

The Imperative of Guiding Teenagers in Goal-Setting: A Biblical Perspective

In a rapidly changing society, it is of paramount importance for teenagers to develop a vision for their future. It's during these formative years that life goals are often formulated, refined, or even discarded. While teenagers are charged with the task of self-discovery, parents have a crucial role to play in aiding their adolescents in establishing meaningful goals that are both challenging and achievable.

The Biblical Principle of Diligence and Planning

Scripture places great emphasis on the importance of planning and diligence. For example, Proverbs 21:5 says, "*The plans of the diligent lead surely to abundance, but everyone who is hasty comes only to poverty.*" (UASV) This wisdom is not merely practical but also deeply spiritual. *Setting and achieving goals are spiritual exercises that, if done wisely, can bring glory to Jehovah and contribute to the advancement of His will on earth.*

The Role of Parents in Goal-Setting

In the formative years, especially the tumultuous years of adolescence, parental guidance in setting appropriate goals is vital. In Ephesians 6:4, we read, "*Fathers, do not provoke your children to anger, but bring them up in the discipline and instruction of the Lord.*" This 'discipline and instruction' includes helping teenagers form realistic and purposeful goals.

Parents as Counselors and Sounding Boards

It's important for parents to serve as wise counselors and sounding boards for their teenagers. This guidance aligns with the principle found in Proverbs 15:22: "*Without counsel plans fail, but with many advisers, they succeed.*" While the teenager should be allowed the freedom to dream and envision, *the parent provides the much-needed practicality that aligns those dreams with Biblical principles and achievable steps.*

The Need for Spiritual Goals

Setting spiritual goals is paramount. In Matthew 6:33, Jesus states, "*But seek first the kingdom of God and his righteousness, and all these things will be added to you.*" Parents should guide their teenagers to place spiritual goals at the forefront. This could include regular participation in church activities, building a solid prayer life, and engaging in evangelistic efforts. *Focusing on spiritual goals often provides the framework within which other goals—academic, vocational, social—can be wisely developed.*

Distinguishing Between Short-Term and Long-Term Goals

Parents must help teenagers understand the difference between short-term and long-term goals, as well as how short-term goals can contribute to the achievement of long-term objectives. Proverbs 6:6-8 praises the ant for its foresight and planning, suggesting that we too should think both immediately and well into the future.

Building a Future Rooted in Biblical Principles

In summary, goal-setting is a multi-faceted endeavor that has profound implications for a teenager's spiritual, emotional, and professional well-being. Scriptural principles clearly support this important part of human development. By actively engaging with their teenagers in this area, parents are fulfilling their God-given role as mentors and guides. They are equipping their young ones not only to succeed in the world but also to be faithful servants of God, thus realizing the most important goal of all: "Well done, good and faithful servant. You have been faithful over a little; I will set you over much. Enter into the joy of your master" (Matthew 25:21).

The Importance of Making Teenagers Feel Needed and Important

One of the essential aspects of child-rearing, especially during the critical years of adolescence, is to make teenagers feel needed and important. This doesn't mean fostering a sense of entitlement or overinflating their ego, but rather imbuing them with a sense of purpose and value that aligns with Biblical principles.

Biblical Foundation for Individual Worth

Let's first establish the Scriptural basis for this idea. The Bible emphasizes the intrinsic worth of every individual, created in the image of God (Genesis 1:27). Each person has a unique role in the fulfillment of God's will (Romans 12:4-8). Knowing that one has been fearfully and wonderfully made (Psalm 139:14) should encourage parents to pass on this sense of worth to their teenagers.

Emotional and Spiritual Stability

Emotional Benefits: When teenagers feel needed and important, they are more likely to develop self-confidence and a balanced sense of self-esteem, grounded in their identity in Christ (Galatians 2:20).

Spiritual Benefits: A sense of purpose can encourage spiritual growth. Knowing that they have a role in the body of Christ can encourage teens to cultivate their gifts (1 Peter 4:10).

Practical Steps to Make Your Teenager Feel Needed and Important

1. Assign Responsibilities

Whether it's a household chore, a service at the church, or any other task where their unique skills can be applied, make it their responsibility. This not only teaches them accountability but also the Biblical principle of stewardship (Matthew 25:14-30).

2. Involve Them in Decision Making

This is a subtle yet effective way of showing them that their opinion is valued. Of course, the final decision rests with the parents, who are the God-appointed authorities in the home (Ephesians 6:1-4), but involving teenagers in the process teaches them wisdom and discernment.

3. Celebrate Their Achievements, However Small

Acknowledgment and celebration reinforce the idea that they are valuable. This can be as simple as praising them for good behavior or as significant as celebrating milestones like academic achievements. "A word fitly spoken is like apples of gold in pictures of silver" (Proverbs 25:11).

4. Quality Time and Open Communication

Spend quality time with your teenagers. Discuss their aspirations, concerns, and feelings. The Bible emphasizes the importance of wise counsel and open communication (Proverbs 15:22).

5. Point Them to Scriptural Heroes

The Bible is filled with examples of young individuals who made a significant impact, like Joseph, David, and Timothy. Highlight these stories to show that God can use them at their age for His glory.

The Risks of Neglecting This Need

Failing to make teenagers feel needed and important can result in a host of negative outcomes: a lack of motivation, spiritual lethargy, and even a susceptibility to ungodly influences who might exploit their need for validation.

In summary, making your teenager feel needed and important is not just a psychological need but also a spiritual imperative. As stewards of God's gifts, including our children, it is our duty to cultivate in them a balanced sense of worth and purpose, rooted and grounded in the Word of God.

Guiding Through Early Adulthood: The Necessity of Wisdom in Parenting

The late teenage years and the transition into early adulthood are seminal periods in a young person's life. It is a phase replete with decisions that could shape the trajectory of their entire future—be it spiritually, emotionally, or professionally. Therefore, it is crucial for parents to provide guidance that is both nurturing and rooted in wisdom.

The Scriptural Foundation of Wisdom

The Bible places immense value on wisdom as an attribute to be sought after and cherished. Proverbs 4:7 states, "Wisdom is the principal thing; therefore get wisdom. And in all your getting, get understanding." This isn't just good advice; it's a directive from Jehovah, who values wisdom so highly that He is described as the "only wise God" (1 Timothy 1:17). Acquiring and applying godly wisdom is an act of obedience and a means of drawing closer to our Creator.

Individual Choices in the Framework of Godly Wisdom

It is essential to remember that as much as you want to guide your child, they are individual souls responsible for their own choices. As you guide them, always let your counsel be tinged with the humility that acknowledges their individuality. You are not dictating their path; rather, you are offering a framework within which they can make godly decisions. Galatians 6:5 reinforces this idea by stating, "For each one will bear his own load."

Practical Advice Balanced with Spiritual Guidance

While it's essential to offer practical advice, say, on career choices, this must always be balanced with spiritual considerations. Jesus reminded us to "seek first the kingdom of God and His righteousness" (Matthew 6:33). Your guidance should reflect this balance, reminding them that while worldly accomplishments are important, they are secondary to their relationship with Jehovah.

Fostering a Climate of Open Communication

It is imperative to create an environment where your emerging adult feels comfortable seeking your counsel. Proverbs 15:22 declares, "Plans fail when there is no counsel, but with many advisers they succeed." Encourage your child to see you as one of these 'advisers,' someone whose experience and wisdom can help them navigate the complexities of early adulthood.

The Importance of Being a Living Example

You can offer all the wise counsel in the world, but if your life does not mirror the wisdom you propose, your words may fall on deaf ears. Paul urged Timothy to be an example "in word, in conduct, in love, in spirit, in faith, in purity" (1 Timothy 4:12). Strive to be that example for your child as well, so your guidance is not just a theoretical construct but a lived reality.

As your child stands on the precipice of early adulthood, your role transitions from that of a caregiver to a wise counselor. This shift should be undertaken with serious consideration and prayerful reflection, always seeking wisdom from Jehovah, "who gives to all generously and without reproach" (James 1:5). By doing so, you offer your child not just earthly guidance but eternal principles that will hold them in good stead all their lives.

The Balancing Act: A Guiding Hand and Room to Grow

The journey through adolescence into adulthood is akin to a path strewn with both obstacles and opportunities. One of the most critical roles for parents during this transitional phase is to offer a guiding hand over life's hurdles while simultaneously allowing teenagers the room to grow, learn, and sometimes even stumble.

Understanding the Role of a Guiding Hand

The wisdom found in Scripture offers a solid foundation for parents to understand their roles as guideposts. Proverbs 22:6 states, "Train up a child in the way he should go, and when he is old he will not depart from it." This verse encapsulates the essence of guidance—equipping the young person for the eventualities of life based on godly principles.

In the Biblical context, Jehovah is often seen as a Shepherd, guiding His flock. Similarly, parents need to adopt the role of shepherds with their children, guiding them through the convoluted paths of life. Guidance doesn't mean steering them according to your will, but according to God's will, as revealed in His word.

Room to Grow and Learn: The Importance of Experience

While guidance is essential, so is the experience that comes with making decisions, facing consequences, and growing from them. Ecclesiastes 3:1 reminds us, "To everything there is a season, a time for every purpose under heaven." There is a time for guidance and a time for independence. To grow and flourish, young people need the opportunity to make decisions for themselves within the boundaries of godly wisdom. Experience can be a powerful teacher, and as they say, some lessons are best learned the hard way.

Fostering Autonomy within a Godly Framework

The objective should be to create an environment where the teenager feels they have the autonomy to make choices, yet understands the importance of making those choices within a framework of Scriptural guidance. Paul's exhortation in Ephesians 6:4 underscores this: "Fathers, do not provoke your children to anger, but bring them up in the discipline and instruction of the Lord."

Navigating the Hurdles of Life

Life will throw numerous challenges—some minor, some potentially life-altering—at your teenager. It's natural to want to shield them from hardship, but keep in mind that Jehovah allows suffering as part of the human condition. This includes the trials your child will face. Rather than protecting them from every obstacle, prepare them to navigate through it. This approach aligns well with Romans 5:3-4, which tells us that "tribulation produces perseverance; and perseverance, character; and character, hope."

Concluding Remarks

Balancing guidance and autonomy is not about finding a middle ground between two extremes; it's about harmoniously integrating both into your parenting strategy. As you guide your child, always keep a prayerful heart, seeking the wisdom that "comes from above" (James 3:17). Your ultimate aim is to prepare them to take on not just the hurdles of life but the responsibilities of a God-fearing adult. By striking this delicate balance, you not only fulfill your role as a parent but also honor Jehovah for the privilege of parenthood.

www.ingramcontent.com/pod-product-compliance
Lightning Source LLC
Chambersburg PA
CBHW022106040426

42451CB00007B/153